Also in this series:

# SHOWTYM ADVENTURES

## CAMEO,
## THE STREET PONY

# CAMEO,
# THE STREET PONY

PUFFIN

UK | USA | Canada | Ireland | Australia
India | New Zealand | South Africa | China

Puffin is an imprint of the Penguin Random House group of companies, whose addresses
can be found at global.penguinrandomhouse.com.

Penguin
Random House
New Zealand

First published by Penguin Random House New Zealand, 2018

10 9 8 7 6 5 4 3 2 1

Text © Kelly Wilson, 2018

The moral right of the author has been asserted.

Design by Cat Taylor © Penguin Random House New Zealand
Illustrations by Heather Wilson © Penguin Random House New Zealand
Cover illustrations by Jenny Cooper © Penguin Random House New Zealand

Printed and bound in Australia by Griffin Press, an Accredited ISO AS/NZS 14001
Environmental Management Systems Printer

A catalogue record for this book is available from the National Library of New Zealand.

ISBN 978-0-14-377220-0
eISBN 978-0-14-377221-7

penguinrandomhouse.co.nz

This book is dedicated to my elder sister, Vicki.

Thank you for constantly inspiring our love of horses and teaching us how to dream. You have always been our biggest supporter and our greatest role model; in our eyes you have always been a champion. Without you, Amanda and I wouldn't be the riders we are today, and we are forever grateful for everything you have taught us over the years.

Growing up, we Wilson sisters — Vicki, Amanda and me (I'm Kelly) —
were three ordinary girls with a love of horses and dreams of Grand Prix
show jumping, taming wild horses and becoming world champions.

In *Showtym Adventures*, we want to share stories based on our early
years with ponies, to inspire you to have big dreams, too! I hope you
enjoy reading about the special ponies that started us on our journey...

Love,
   Kelly

# Contents

# Chapter 1
# Street Pony

"You went to hospital and you're coming home with a pony?" Kelly almost dropped the phone in disbelief. Mum had been in hospital for a week, after having an operation. But surely she had spent the entire time lying in bed, recovering . . . ? "When did you even have time to look at ponies?"

"I saw her from my window. She was trotting down the main street of town, towed behind a rusty old truck," Mum replied down the phone.

"Now I know you're making up stories," Kelly laughed. She wandered into the kitchen and pulled the pantry door open. The cupboard was looking frightfully bare. With a sigh she pulled out half a dozen stale crackers and placed them on the kitchen bench.

"I'm serious!" Mum said. "The nurse knew the guy who owned the pony. I called him, and he agreed to sell her. Now, put your dad on the line. I need him to bring the horse truck when he picks me up tomorrow."

Kelly headed outside to find her dad. "Mum wants to talk to you," she said as she passed the phone over. "I think the surgery is making her imagine things."

ᴗ ᴗ ᴗ

The next morning Kelly and her sisters were running late for school. The past week had been hard without their mum, and Vicki, Kelly's older sister, was no help.

"I don't understand how you can burn toast," Kelly complained as the smoke alarm sounded. "You're two years older than me! How come you're no good at cooking, or cleaning, or helping Amanda get dressed?" She glanced down at their little sister, who was trying to tie her laces. "She's got her shoes on the wrong feet again."

"Luckily I have other talents," Vicki said with a grin, and bent to fix Amanda's shoes. "I'd rather be outside with the horses any day."

The loud wailing had brought Dad running. He grabbed a tea towel and waved it in the direction of the alarm.

"That's three days in a row you've burnt something!" he yelled above the noise. "You need to be more careful!" The alarm fell silent and he turned to the mess in the kitchen. "Here, let me throw some food together. You'll have to eat while I drive, or you'll be late again."

Ten minutes later the sisters piled out the door in their school uniforms, bags in one hand and a sandwich in the other. Dad was waiting by their little horse truck.

"Climb in, girls," he said, opening the door for them. "I'll drop you off and carry on to get Mum."

"I thought she was kidding when she said she'd bought a new pony," Kelly said as she did up her seat belt.

"So did I," Dad said. "But apparently, for three hundred and fifty dollars, we are the proud owners of a pony she has only seen from a distance."

∪ ∪ ∪

As soon as the bell sounded for the end of the day, Kelly and her sisters rushed to the school gate where their dad was waiting for them.

"Tell us about the new pony," Amanda squealed.

"You are going to love her," he replied. "But I'm sworn to secrecy. Mum will answer all your questions as soon as we're home."

"At least tell us who she's for," Vicki begged him.

"Nope. I promised."

As they drove home, the sisters argued over the new pony's size and colour, and who would get to ride it. Kelly was positive it wasn't for Vicki — only a year earlier she'd tamed a wild mountain pony called Just Fine 'n' Dandy. At their first show together, months earlier, they'd won lots of ribbons.

But Kelly was sure it couldn't be for her or Amanda, either. They both had little 11-hands-high grey ponies, Twinkle and Charlie, which they loved. Even Mum had her own horse now, having tamed Jude, another wild pony they'd rounded up at the same time as Dandy. That left only one person.

"Is the new pony for you, Dad?" Kelly asked.

He smiled and shook his head as he turned into their long gravel driveway. "She's much too small for me! She's 13.2 hands — the same height as Dandy."

The girls could barely wait for the car to stop before jumping out in search of their mum. They found her on the porch, resting.

"Where's the pony?" Amanda asked, looking around.

"It's good to see you, too!" Mum said. "A whole week without me, and all you're interested in is horses?"

"I'm glad you're back — and I'm getting tired of cooking," Kelly said, as she wrapped her mum in a hug. "You're lucky we survived at all, with Vicki and Dad's attempts."

"That's not fair, Kelly," Dad's voice came from behind them. "My corn fritters were edible."

Kelly spun around, ready to argue, and froze. There on the driveway beside her father was a striking grey pony. Unlike Twinkle and Charlie, who were almost white, the mare's coat was the colour of steel. She had four long white stockings and a blaze contrasting with her dark grey coat.

"She looks like she's from a painting!" Kelly said, as soon as she could speak. "She's the prettiest pony I've ever seen."

"You say that about every pony," Vicki teased her. She stepped closer to pat the mare. "Mum, what's her name?"

"She doesn't have one. I thought—"

"Who doesn't name their pony?" Kelly gasped. "The poor thing!"

"She's four years old and was apparently born in the bush. The guy hadn't owned her for long. He didn't own a horse trailer, either, so to move her to new grazing he tied her to the back of his truck and towed her along. That's why I spotted her on the main street."

"I truly thought you were joking when you told me that. Didn't she mind all the cars, and the people?" Kelly asked.

"She was as quiet as a lamb," Mum replied. "My point, though — before you distracted me, Kelly —

was that I thought *you* should name her."

"Why me?"

"Because, if you like her, she's yours." Mum smiled at the look on Kelly's face. "You're starting to look like a giant on Twinkle. Now that you're nine, you need something bigger."

Giving her mum another hug, Kelly walked slowly to her new pony and studied her closely. She looked like she'd never been groomed in her life. Her steel-grey coat was dull, her hooves were cracked and her tail, which was so long it brushed the ground, was knotted with leaves and twigs. But Kelly also noticed the gentle expression in her eyes

and the prick of her ears. "I love her," she declared, patting her head. The young mare stood calmly, even though she was now surrounded by the entire family. "Since she's as pretty as a picture, what about Cameo for her name?"

"What's a cameo?" Amanda asked.

"You know, like those beautiful paintings in the old brooches Nana wears."

Cameo nuzzled Kelly, seemingly in approval.

"I think you're her favourite already," Vicki said. "She didn't do that when I patted her."

"She's the sweetest pony I've ever met," Kelly said with a giggle. She whispered in Cameo's ear, "I hope you're as kind as you seem. I'm not the bravest rider but, if you look after me, I promise we'll have lots of fun adventures together."

She untangled a dreadlock in Cameo's unkempt mane. "As soon as I've groomed her, I'll take her for a ride."

"Oh, you'll be able to do that one day soon, I'm sure," said Mum, suddenly looking guilty. "But there's something I forgot to mention: Cameo has never been ridden."

# Chapter 2
# Cameo's List

Startled, Kelly looked up at her parents. "If she hasn't been ridden, what am I supposed to do with her?"

"That's a good question," Dad said. He was frowning at Mum, and seemed equally surprised that the new pony was unbroken.

"I thought Vicki could help Kelly train her. She could put into practice all the lessons she learned working with Dandy last summer," Mum explained.

Fear filled Kelly's stomach. When she was seven, she'd had a bad fall off a horse at Pony Club camp and had had to wear a neck brace. Then last year she had been kicked by Dandy. After that, she had been reluctant to ride any pony except her trusty mare, Twinkle.

She shook her head. "I don't think I'm brave enough," she said, unable to stop tears of disappointment rushing into her eyes. "I'm too scared of getting hurt again!"

"It'll be OK, Kelly, I'll help you," Vicki said, putting an arm around her sister. "Make a list of everything you need Cameo to learn before you'd feel safe riding her, and I'll train her for you."

"But that could be months away," Kelly said, wiping her eyes. "And what will Dandy do while you train Cameo?"

"I'll ride him in the mornings before school, so I have enough time in the evenings for Cameo." Vicki shrugged. "It'll all work out. You can help me with jobs so that I have enough time."

Looking over at her parents, Kelly was relieved to see them nodding in agreement.

"You'll have to look after her, though," Mum said. "Vicki might be helping you train her, but in every other way Cameo is your responsibility."

"I can do that," Kelly promised and wrapped her arms around Cameo's neck. "When can we start?"

"How about right now?" Dad said. "The sooner Cameo's training begins, the sooner you'll be riding her."

∪ ∪ ∪

Kelly dashed into the house to grab a piece of paper and a pen, then joined Amanda and her parents at the fence to watch Vicki and Cameo in the paddock. Vicki was asking the pony to lunge around her in a circle, and Cameo was clearly confused.

"She doesn't know anything," Kelly wailed.

Mum leapt to Cameo's defence. "That's not true. She's good to catch and lead, and she was very easy to load on the truck."

"OK — compared to a wild pony she knows a lot, but in comparison to Twinkle she's as green as grass," Kelly said. "Does she even know how to pick up her hooves for a trim?"

Her mum's face went blank. "I never thought to ask. I guess we'll find out soon enough."

Kelly let out a sigh of exasperation, and started making her list for Vicki. There was certainly lots that the new pony needed to learn.

"Dad, would you help me with Cameo? I think she's ready for me to lie over her back," Vicki said twenty minutes later, once the young mare had settled down.

Kelly held her breath as her dad slowly boosted her sister up. Vicki quietly lay over Cameo's back. Only part of her weight was on the mare; the rest was still supported by her dad. Cameo shifted her weight uneasily but held her ground, nuzzling Dad for reassurance.

"She seems easier than Dandy," Kelly said as soon as Vicki jumped back to the ground.

"Yes, she's definitely not like a wild stallion," Vicki laughed. "Dandy took off the first time I tried this with him!"

"I think she'll make a lovely pony for you, Kelly," her dad said encouragingly. "You just need to be a bit patient."

Even though Cameo was being asked to do new things, she was showing all the signs of being completely relaxed. Her ears were pricked forward and, as Kelly watched her, the docile mare blinked slowly, gazing back.

"She doesn't seem very bothered by us," Kelly said, and reached forward to pat Cameo's forehead.

"She is very trusting," Vicki agreed.

Kelly stepped back as her dad legged Vicki up again. This time Vicki rested her full weight on the mare, holding a handful of mane to stay balanced.

"Would you try walking her in a circle?" Vicki asked her dad.

Kelly watched nervously as Cameo took her first step with Vicki lying like a sack of potatoes over her withers. Vicki had never gotten to this stage with Dandy — every time the stallion felt her weight, he'd leapt forward and she'd fallen to the ground. It was only after sending him to a professional trainer for two weeks that he'd become safe enough for her to ride.

Cameo, though, slowly circled the paddock behind their dad, before coming to a halt. Although she had been hesitant, she hadn't misbehaved and Vicki reached forward and patted the mare's neck.

Kelly finally let out her breath as she watched her sister slide off Cameo's back.

"That's probably enough for today," Mum called from the fence.

"Cameo did so well," Kelly beamed, running over to give her pony a pat.

"She's going to be lovely," Vicki said. "I'll work with her each day, for as long as you want."

Kelly pulled the piece of paper from her pocket and passed it to her sister. "I wrote this while I was watching you. It's what I'd like you to teach her."

## What Cameo Knows:
- How to be caught
- How to lead
- How to load on the horse truck

## What Cameo Needs To Know:
- How to pick up her hooves?
- How to halt and turn with a rider
- How to walk, trot and canter bareback
- How to be ridden in a saddle and bridle
- How to jump over logs
- How to be ridden on the farm with other ponies

As Vicki read through the list, a smile spread across her face.

"Too easy," she said. "She'll be ready for you in no time."

Kelly wished she could feel as confident as her sister.

# Chapter 3
# Challenge Accepted

THE NEXT AFTERNOON KELLY HEADED down to the paddock to catch Cameo, then carefully groomed her until she shone like burnished steel. Though she didn't feel ready to train the grey pony herself, she could still enjoy spending time with her, and she was quickly falling in love with her sweet nature.

"I wish I knew what your life was like before you came to us," Kelly said as she ran her hands down Cameo's leg. She was pleased when the mare lifted her hoof. "So you *do* know how to pick up your hooves. I wonder why no one's trimmed them?"

Cracks split the hoof walls, and Kelly had to work hard to loosen stones that had pushed their way into them.

That done, Kelly ran to get the trimming gear, and went down the driveway in search of Mum. "I picked up Cameo's hooves and she was really good," she said proudly. "I was wondering if you could trim them?"

"Good idea," Mum said.

Kelly watched carefully as Cameo's hooves were tidied up. Then she went to find Vicki. It was time to continue her pony's training.

"Ready to cross some things off Cameo's list?"

Vicki nodded eagerly. "We can practise stopping and turning today. Then if she's ready, I'm hoping Dad will let me ride her off the lead rein."

Kelly wished she could be as brave as her sister — how special it would be to train Cameo all by herself. But as soon as the thought crossed her mind, it flashed back to the fall at Pony Club, and how she'd ended up in hospital. She quickly handed Vicki Cameo's rope.

"I'll get Mum and Dad and Amanda. They won't want to miss this," she said. "We'll meet you in the front paddock."

∪ ∪ ∪

"Do you want me to hold her again?" Dad asked as Vicki led the young mare towards them.

"Yes, please," Vicki said. "Let's start by repeating what Cameo learnt yesterday."

Kelly watched as Cameo stood quietly while Vicki lay across her back. Within a few minutes Vicki was sitting upright on Cameo, stroking her neck.

"Are you sure she hasn't been ridden before? She's so easy, I feel like I'm sitting on Charlie," Vicki joked, referring to Amanda's quiet grey pony.

"He's not easy," Amanda frowned. "The other day he shook his head and I fell off."

Vicki sighed. "That was because you didn't groom him properly and he had bits of hay under his saddle blanket."

"I'm positive she hasn't been ridden," Mum cut in, as Amanda poked out her tongue. "But she's had a lot of life experience for such a young pony. After trotting through the streets, I doubt this is very stressful for her."

For the next half-hour Kelly took note of

everything Vicki did with Cameo, so that she could one day do the same thing. First, Vicki asked Cameo to turn her head, while standing still, to each side. Then they practised walking on the lead rein, with Vicki gently pulling back on both reins to teach her how to stop.

At first Cameo was very unsure about moving forward with Vicki on her back and swung her head from side to side in confusion. Kelly watched anxiously as the mare's ears flicked backwards and forwards, her movements stilted.

"I can't believe you thought it was a good idea to buy me a young pony," Kelly told her mother. "I'd be freaking out right now if I was riding her."

"Give her a chance, Kelly," Mum said. "Every pony has to start somewhere. I have a feeling that one day Cameo will be as quiet to ride as she is to handle."

Unconvinced, Kelly's gaze returned to Cameo only to find that the pony had settled and was now striding out, slow and steady. Vicki drew Cameo back to a halt, and her father unclipped the lead and stepped away.

With no person to follow, Cameo was a little

unsure at first, but Vicki patiently guided the mare. In no time at all they were circling the paddock and changing direction.

"We've crossed the second task off your list! What's next?" Vicki said, as she brought Cameo to a halt and leapt to the ground. Jolted by the sudden movement, Cameo snorted and stepped sideways, watching Vicki warily.

Kelly pulled out her sheet of paper. "To complete the second task, you need to trot and canter."

"Let's give her a couple more days to get used to a rider, then I'm sure she she'll be ready for your next challenge," Mum said, reaching out and patting Cameo.

U U U

Over the next two days, Kelly watched with pride as Cameo's confidence grew. At the end of the young mare's third ride with Vicki, she was looking relaxed and Kelly was sure she was ready for the next task on her list.

"Maybe you can try a little trot before you finish?"

Kelly asked her sister.

Vicki looked at her parents for permission, and asked Cameo forward again.

Once the mare was walking confidently, she squeezed her heels against Cameo's side to ask for a trot.

Nothing.

Again Vicki urged Cameo forward, this time giving her a little kick, but the mare didn't understand and maintained a steady walk. Nothing Vicki tried could entice Cameo to increase her speed. Kelly could see that Vicki was at a loss — her own pony, Dandy, loved going fast.

"Ideas, anyone?" Vicki finally asked, halting Cameo by the fence.

"She was happy trotting behind the truck," Mum said thoughtfully. "Maybe she would be happier following someone?"

"I'll run in front of her," Kelly said eagerly. She climbed through the fence and rubbed Cameo between the eyes. "You ready, girl?" she whispered.

Turning around, she started forward in a slow jog. Behind her, Kelly could hear Cameo's hoof-beats change from the four-beat pace of a walk to the faster two-beats of a trot. Glancing back, she caught a glimpse of the mare's ears pricked forward as Cameo kept pace with her.

Vicki quietly closed her fingers on the reins, asking the mare to slow down. Cameo, happy to have a break, fell back into a walk and then halted.

Vicki dismounted and patted her. Cameo tossed her head. She clearly had enjoyed the trot.

"She was amazing!" Vicki said, stroking Cameo's neck. "Let's try one more time, and this time run as fast as you possibly can."

Taking off at a run, Kelly strained her legs to sprint faster than she ever had before. Focused on her speed, and trying not to trip over the uneven ground, she didn't notice the change in Cameo's hoof beats.

"She's cantering," Vicki breathed in awe.

Convinced her sister was joking, Kelly looked back. Sure enough, Cameo was cantering behind her.

Kelly slowed to a walk and bent over to catch her breath while Cameo halted beside her. She wrapped her arms around Cameo's neck and, as soon as she could speak, said, "Your first trot and canter bareback! That's three things crossed off our list. It won't be long till I'm riding you!"

"If you want to have a quick ride, I think she'd be OK if I lead you." Vicki said, dismounting and patting Cameo. "We could just go for a short walk."

Kelly shook her head, once again nervous. "I wouldn't know what to do if something went wrong."

"What about just sitting on her while she's standing still?"

Kelly bit her lip.

"You really need to live a little," Vicki said, rolling her eyes.

"Complete the list. Once you've proven she's safe, I'll be happy to ride her," Kelly said firmly. "Until then, I'll keep riding Twinkle."

## What Cameo Needs To Know:

- ~~How to pick up her hooves?~~
- ~~How to halt and turn with a rider~~
- ~~How to walk, trot and canter bareback~~
- How to be ridden in a saddle and bridle
- How to jump over logs
- How to be ridden on the farm with other ponies

# Chapter 4
# Follow the Leader

THE NEXT MORNING WAS SATURDAY. Kelly woke her sisters at dawn, eager to see Cameo again. "Come on, guys, let's make the most of the weekend. No sleeping in!"

With a yawn, Amanda rolled over. "Who are you, and what have you done with my sister?"

"You hate mornings," Vicki grumbled in agreement. "How come you're awake so early?"

"I had an idea. Since Cameo likes to follow, I thought we could play Follow the Leader. I'll ride Twinkle and you can shadow us everywhere!"

Vicki sat up. "That's actually a brilliant idea!"

"Can I play, too?" Amanda asked.

"How about you watch today? Then, if Cameo copes, you can join in tomorrow."

Amanda wrinkled her nose in protest and snuggled deep under the covers. Kelly could hear her muffled grumbling all the way to the kitchen.

She waited impatiently while Vicki changed into her riding clothes, and then they had a hurried breakfast and headed outside.

Kelly bent over to pull on her jodhpur boots. "Last one to have their pony ready is a rotten egg!" she yelled, and took off at a sprint towards Twinkle's paddock.

υ υ υ

The next week flew by, and each day Kelly saw an improvement in Cameo. The sisters continued playing Follow the Leader, with Amanda joining in on Charlie, and found all sorts of unusual places to ride. Soon Cameo was confident going down banks, jumping across ditches, walking over logs and riding through puddles on the driveway. Vicki had even progressed from riding Cameo bareback, with a halter, to riding her with a saddle and bridle.

That weekend, Kelly woke early once again. Vicki had said Cameo might be ready for her first farm ride, and Kelly couldn't wait to see how she would cope in a group of ponies.

"Come on, Vicki," Kelly said, shaking her sister awake. "Let's go! I can't wait to see another thing crossed off Cameo's list!"

"It's Saturday," Vicki grumbled. "I've been up at six every day before school to ride Dandy — I need a sleep-in!"

"Sorry," said Kelly, full of remorse. In her eagerness to make progress, she had forgotten how much extra work her sister had been putting in trying to work both ponies each day.

"Why don't you go saddle up, and then come get me once Cameo's ready?" Vicki yawned, as she climbed out of bed and rummaged through her drawers for clothes.

Kelly and Amanda headed outside to catch their ponies. Their dad joined them soon after. He'd promised to ride out on Jude to make sure they stayed safe, since Mum was still too sore after her surgery.

Soon all four ponies were caught and groomed, with their hooves picked out.

Kelly led Cameo down to the house to meet Vicki. Holding the end of Cameo's rope, she climbed the steps onto the porch, opened the front door and stepped inside.

"Vicki, Cameo's ready for you," she called.

Behind her, Kelly heard a clip-clop of hooves and swung around in surprise. The curious mare had climbed the steps and followed her inside.

"Kelly!" Mum yelled. "Why is your pony in the house?"

"The better question," Vicki replied, emerging from the bedroom, her hair pulled back into a messy ponytail, "is how are we going to get her out?"

Kelly looked around. Their tiny house wasn't made for ponies, and looked even smaller with Cameo in it. There wasn't enough room to turn around, and backing her through the door and down the steps seemed just as hazardous.

"It'll be a tight squeeze," Mum said, moving chairs and clothes out of the way, "but I think we could lead her out through the French doors."

Carefully Kelly inched Cameo forward, through the kitchen and living room, which also doubled up as her parents' bedroom, and out the far doorway onto the deck. She heaved a sigh of relief when Cameo was safely back on solid ground.

"I think we need to add 'Teach Cameo to stay' to the list," Kelly laughed, as she handed the rope to Vicki, and headed off to get Twinkle.

Five minutes later, Kelly and Twinkle led the way up the driveway and onto the road, careful to keep on the grass verge. A truck drove past and Cameo didn't even flinch. Kelly caught her sister's eye and smiled — the pony was in her element on the streets.

They crossed the old wooden bridge and rode up the driveway to the neighbouring farmer's gate. Kelly jumped off Twinkle to open it, waiting until the last pony was through before re-latching the gate behind them.

"Let's take it slowly until we're sure Cameo's going to behave," Dad cautioned.

"OK," Vicki agreed. "Kelly, why don't we go up the first hill together, then if she's good we'll try the next one as a group."

To Kelly's delight, Vicki and Cameo quietly cantered behind her and Twinkle up the hill without tugging on the reins or trying to go faster, and then the four of them stood quietly at the top as they waited for the others to catch up. It had only been ten days since Cameo had arrived at their property, but now, for the first time, Kelly could imagine riding her.

"How was she?" Amanda called out as she cantered Charlie towards them. Her legs were flying as she urged her pony faster, but the little grey was tired and fell back to a walk.

"Perfect," Kelly grinned proudly. "She was absolutely perfect."

"Can Charlie and I join you on the next hill?"

Vicki nodded. "Let's all canter up together."

∪ ∪ ∪

Over the next few days, as Vicki continued to ride Cameo, Kelly's impatience to ride her new pony began to outweigh her fears.

"You should jump Cameo today," Kelly said as

they were driven home from school. "Then you will have taught Cameo everything on the list. Maybe tomorrow I can ride her for the first time."

"Are you sure?" Vicki asked. "It's only been two weeks, so she's still pretty inexperienced."

"I think I'm ready," Kelly said. "I wasn't brave enough at first, but after seeing how kind she is my confidence has grown."

"Even I'd feel safe on her," Amanda said, with an exaggerated sigh. "She's the quietest pony ever."

"Before anyone does any riding, don't forget you promised to pull out weeds from the horses' paddocks," Mum said from the front seat. The girls all groaned; when it came to owning ponies, the jobs never stopped.

∪ ∪ ∪

Two hours later Kelly and her sisters were sitting with their feet dangling over the river bank, watching for eels. Beside them stood three large sacks full of ragwort and buttercup that they'd pulled out. Both plants were poisonous to horses, so the girls always kept an eye on the paddocks to get rid of any weeds that popped up.

"So who do you think pulled the most weeds today?" Amanda asked, sizing up the sacks. "I think I got as many as you guys today."

"I think I might have, but only just," Kelly said, lifting each to see which was heaviest.

They carried the sacks back to the house, so their dad could burn the weeds on a bonfire. They were always careful to never leave the weeds somewhere the horses could eat them, or on the ground in case the seeds caused more weeds to grow.

"Mum!" Kelly called out from the doorway, as Amanda darted towards the kitchen, leaving muddy footprints across the floor. "We're done! Is it all right if we ride to the reserve so Cameo can jump logs? It's the final thing on her list!"

Their mum appeared around the corner, taking in Vicki and Kelly's grubby fingers and sparkling eyes. "Of course it is. You'll have to let me know how she goes! Did you fill up one sack each?"

"Right to the top," Amanda said from behind, her mouth full of food. "That's a dollar each, right?"

Mum's eyes narrowed as she traced the muddy

trail. "Oh Amanda," she sighed. "Look at the mess you've made."

Amanda flashed her a grin, ducked under her arm and stepped outside. "Luckily, you love me anyway."

Shaking her head, Mum reached into her pocket and drew out three gold coins.

Kelly took her share of the money carefully. "Thanks, Mum! To celebrate Cameo and Vicki finishing the list we'll buy some lollies at the dairy."

Ten minutes later, Kelly and her sisters were heading up the road on their ponies. To save time, they'd all decided to ride bareback; even Vicki, who was going to try her first jump on Cameo.

When they reached the reserve, they cantered their ponies along the winding path through the trees. Twinkle and Charlie took the lead, leaping over logs and branches they'd made into makeshift jumps a few months earlier. Vicki followed closely behind on Cameo, the brave little pony clearing every obstacle in her path.

"She's amazing," Kelly said when they reached the end of the trail. "I can't believe we crossed everything off the list in just two weeks. I thought it would be months before I could ride her. I think she might actually be the best pony in the world."

Laughing, Vicki gave the young mare a pat. "Second best, maybe. Out of loyalty I have to argue Dandy is the best."

"Don't you listen to them," Amanda leant forward to whisper in Charlie's ear. "You are better than them all."

Turning the ponies back down the hill, they cantered over the logs one more time before carrying on towards the dairy to spend their hard-earned money. With every step that passed, Kelly's anticipation grew. Now the list was completed there was nothing to stop her from riding Cameo.

## What Cameo Needs To Know:

- ~~How to pick up her hooves?~~
- ~~How to halt and turn with a rider~~
- ~~How to walk, trot and canter bareback~~
- ~~How to be ridden in a saddle and bridle~~
- ~~How to jump over logs~~
- ~~How to be ridden on the farm with other ponies~~

# Chapter 5
# Kelly's Turn

KELLY WOKE ON SATURDAY MORNING feeling equal parts nervous and excited. Now that she was only a few hours away from riding Cameo for the first time, her tummy was filled with butterflies, and she wished she'd waited a little while longer before begging to ride her.

"You ready?" Amanda asked, as they finished cleaning their saddles and bridles.

Sick to her stomach, Kelly nodded. "I'm a little nervous," she confessed, "but I really do want to ride her today."

"You'll love Cameo," Vicki said from behind them. "I bet you could cross everything off your list all in one ride, if you wanted to!"

"You mean I'd have to ride her bareback, and canter and jump?" Kelly said, nervously chewing on her lip. "I was thinking just a quiet walk in the paddock."

"Well, if you're too scared, I'll ride her," Amanda said cheekily.

Kelly glared at Amanda. "No, I'm not! How about I do all that but use a saddle? Then tomorrow I'll ride her bareback."

"Deal," Vicki said with a grin. "I'm looking forward to riding Dandy out with everyone again. I bet he's been feeling pretty neglected."

∪ ∪ ∪

An hour later, Kelly stood beside her pony. Everyone else, including their mum, was mounted and waiting, but suddenly the thought of riding Cameo seemed overwhelming.

"Are you sure she's ready?" Kelly said, playing

for time. "Because if you don't think she's going to behave I can wait . . ."

"Hurry up and get on your pony," Vicki said sternly. "You're going to love riding Cameo — you just need to give her a chance."

Kelly placed a tentative foot in the stirrup and swung herself up into the saddle. The mare didn't move a muscle, and Kelly relaxed a little. Reaching down, she patted Cameo's neck and whispered, "Be nice to me, girl."

As they made their way down the driveway and along the road, Kelly kept a firm grip on the reins, prepared for something to go wrong. Not used to having such a tight hold, Cameo jig-jogged and tossed her head, tugging the reins from Kelly's hands.

"Vicki, she's playing up," Kelly said tensely. "Can we swap?"

"Your reins are too short," Vicki calmly instructed. "Loosen them so she can stretch out her head."

"But what if she takes off?"

"She's the most laid-back pony ever. She's not going anywhere. Trust me."

Slowly, Kelly lengthened her reins, and soon

Cameo was walking calmly. Kelly let out a huge sigh of relief.

"I think we should just walk today," she said firmly.

"Let's see how things go," Mum replied from the back of the group, on Jude. "Now that you've relaxed, Cameo is perfectly fine."

When they reached the first hill, Kelly was determined to walk up it, but Vicki was equally adamant that Cameo would be fine to trot. Even though Cameo had been well behaved so far, Kelly couldn't stop herself imagining all the things that could go wrong.

"Come on," Vicki said as she trotted off, with Amanda following closely behind. "Keep up."

"I don't want to," Kelly told her mum, shortening Cameo's reins to prevent her following Dandy and Charlie up the hill.

Mum said in a gentle voice, "Kelly, I really believe you can do this. You need to trust Cameo and trust yourself."

"But what if I hurt myself again?" Kelly whispered.

"Oh, honey, what if you don't? You can't live life always expecting the worst. Sometimes you have to try new things, even when it scares you."

"How about just a couple of strides of trot?" Kelly bargained.

"On one condition," her mum said as she urged Jude forward. "If Cameo doesn't do anything wrong, you'll trot again straight away, this time a little further."

Kelly nodded, but when Cameo moved to follow, fear filled her. She really didn't feel ready to trot yet, but she was worried Cameo would misbehave if she got left behind.

Loosening the reins, she let Cameo's head go and sat quietly, letting the pony choose her own pace as she followed Jude up the hill. For the first few metres she walked quietly, then, as the distance between them increased, Cameo broke into the most comfortable, floating trot that Kelly had ever sat on.

Stride after stride, Kelly's fear was slowly replaced with enjoyment, and by the time she caught up to her mum she couldn't contain her smile.

"That wasn't so bad, was it?" Mum asked when they came to a stop.

"She's amazing!" Kelly laughed, as she threw her arms around Cameo's neck to hug her. "I can't believe I was scared! She's so much fun!"

As they rode further around the farm, Kelly's confidence grew, and she sat relaxed in the saddle, chatting to her sisters.

"She's so different to Twinkle," Kelly said thoughtfully.

"She is a lot bigger," Amanda said.

"I mean, her trot's so comfortable," Kelly said. "Twinkle's is so bouncy in comparison."

"Wait until you feel her canter," Vicki said with a grin. "It's even smoother."

Five minutes later, when they reached the top of the big hill in the next paddock over, Kelly couldn't help but agree. Cameo's canter was lovely — she was quite possibly the dreamiest pony Kelly had ever ridden.

"This log would be perfect for you to jump on Cameo," Vicki said as she cantered Dandy towards the felled tree, flying over it.

The log was huge; Kelly had passed it on Twinkle many times, but had never attempted it. Jumping it on Cameo didn't seem any more appealing.

"Don't be silly," Kelly said.

"Come on," Vicki urged. "I bet Cameo will fly

over it. Why don't you just try it, Kelly?"

"Vicki," Mum interrupted with a warning tone. "That's a big log for Kelly's first jump on Cameo. Let's find a smaller one for her to start with."

"Imagine if you jumped it, though," Vicki frowned at Kelly. "You'd feel like you could conquer anything after that."

Kelly shook her head. "I don't want to," she said.

Vicki shrugged her shoulders and spun Dandy around. They were starting for home, when a small, determined voice came from behind them. "I'll do it."

They turned to see Amanda and Charlie cantering towards the log. The tiny grey pony pricked his ears as he approached, then he gathered his legs and soared over, Amanda sitting in perfect balance as he landed. She trotted back to join them, whooping.

"You have to do it now, Kelly, or admit I'm a better rider than you," she grinned slyly.

Although nervous, Kelly was never one to turn down a challenge from her little sister. Squaring her shoulders she considered the log for a long moment, then turned to Vicki and asked, "Would you be able to give me a lead?"

Smiling, Vicki pushed Dandy into a trot and Kelly followed closely behind. Dandy reached the log, gathered himself up and jumped it effortlessly.

At the last minute, when Cameo was just metres from the jump, Kelly grabbed her pony's mane and closed her eyes. Cameo didn't even hesitate. Up and up she flew, clearing the log with room to spare.

"We did it!" Kelly yelled out in joy. "You were amazing, Cameo!"

As they made their way home down the hill, Cameo tugged at the reins, gaining speed as she tried to trot down the hill. Instead of panicking, Kelly leant back and shortened her reins, bringing Cameo back to a walk. After jumping the log, everything seemed much less daunting now.

"Woah there, girl," Kelly said in a firm voice. "None of that silly stuff."

To her delight, Cameo settled instantly, and Kelly was able to relax again. Although Cameo might be young and inexperienced, she had a kind nature. As they made their way home, Kelly imagined all the fun they would have together, jumping at competitions and galloping down the beach.

# Chapter 6
# Triple Trouble

WITH EVERY RIDE KELLY AND Cameo's bond grew stronger, and their confidence grew. Rather than taking the easy routes on the farm, they would venture down animal tracks, jump over ditches and cross rivers. Every log they came to was another chance to improve their jumping. Sometimes Kelly rode out bareback and, one day, when Vicki fell off Dandy after he'd spooked at a tractor driving past and galloped home without her, they'd doubled home together on Cameo.

As Kelly didn't have time to ride two ponies,

Twinkle was sold. Though Kelly was sad to say goodbye to her trusty friend, she knew she had outgrown her and was happy that Twinkle was going to a little girl who would love her for many years to come. While Twinkle would always hold a special place in her heart, Kelly was now looking forward to the future with Cameo.

A few weeks later, Mum asked if they wanted to compete at an upcoming Ribbon Day. All three girls put up their hands, although Kelly was a little hesitant.

"Cameo hasn't even been to Pony Club yet or jumped over proper jumps," she said. "Maybe I should wait until she's had more experience."

"If you're not going to ride her, can I?" Amanda asked.

"Don't be silly, Amanda," Kelly snapped. "If she's not ready for me, then she's not going to be ready for you!"

"Actually, that's not the worst idea," Dad chipped in. "How about you lead Amanda on Cameo in the Lead Rein classes, Kelly? That way she'll get used to being at a show without too much pressure."

"What about Charlie?" Amanda asked. "He

might feel left out. I wouldn't like that."

"I don't think he'll mind staying at home," said Mum. "He can keep Jude company."

Kelly wasn't sure she wanted to share Cameo. She'd secretly been imagining all the ribbons they could win together at their first show.

"Are you sure that's a good idea?"

"For Cameo's first show, I think it would be best for her to just do baby stuff, so she has a good experience," Mum said.

Amanda squealed in delight, then narrowed her eyes. "Baby stuff? I'm not a baby."

"Yes you are," Kelly said, rolling her eyes.

"I'm not. I'm five!"

Her mum and dad shot a warning look, and Kelly clamped her mouth shut. She knew better than to finish the argument in front of them.

∪ ∪ ∪

The morning of the Ribbon Day dawned bright and clear. By 8 a.m. the ponies were caught and loaded into the family's little horse truck, and they began the long drive to the showgrounds. It took almost an hour to drive the winding country roads, and Kelly and her sisters passed the time playing Eye Spy.

As soon as they arrived at the show, though, it was a flurry of activity. While Vicki groomed Dandy to perfection, Amanda and Kelly scrubbed Cameo's white socks with soap, trying to remove the grass stains on her knees.

"I give up," Amanda said, wiping a soapy hand against her brow. "I think that's the cleanest we're going to get her."

"Let's skip the Best Groomed class — there's no way she'll win anyway," Kelly said in defeat.

With that decided, they saddled Cameo, then hopped into the truck to get changed into their Pony Club uniforms.

"Where are your riding boots?" Kelly asked, pointing at the bright red gumboots on Amanda's feet.

"These are my lucky gumboots," Amanda declared. "They'll help us win a red ribbon."

"Mum!" Kelly yelled. "Tell Amanda she can't wear her red gumboots!"

"Amanda, don't you listen to her, you can wear

whatever you like," their mum called back.

Throwing her hands up, Kelly stormed down the ramp to bridle Cameo. Vicki was mounting Dandy, ready for the Best Groomed class. It was only their second show together, as there hadn't been any competitions over the winter, and he was looking better than ever. It was hard to believe he'd been running wild in the mountains only eighteen months before.

"Good luck," Kelly said to her sister. "I wish I could watch, but we're going to be stuck in the Lead Rein ring all morning."

∪ ∪ ∪

Two hours later, the judge tied a second-place ribbon around Cameo's neck for the final class, Best Pony Club Mount.

"I wish I could have ridden her in the Junior Ring," Kelly said, looking at the blue ribbon enviously. Though the morning had been dull and she wished the ribbons were hers to keep, she couldn't be prouder of how Cameo had behaved.

"Then I wouldn't have won all these ribbons," Amanda said, pulling handfuls from her pockets. Then she caught sight of a friend, who was sitting on her little bay pony. Leaping off Cameo, she sprinted away.

"What about helping put her away—" Kelly huffed, but Amanda was already out of earshot. "She's so childish sometimes," Kelly sighed to Cameo as she untied the ribbon from the mare's neck and carefully placed it in her pocket.

As soon as Cameo was watered and had a slice of hay to eat, Kelly headed over to the Junior Ring to watch Vicki. She arrived just in time to see Dandy canter out of the ring with a ribbon around his neck.

"What did you win?"

"Third in Open Pony," Vicki said, as she untied the ribbon and passed it to her mum. "The next class is School Pony, but there's no way Dandy will cope with two people riding him. He's still funny about other people."

The class was a throwback to when their grandparents used to ride to school; two or three riders had to ride in on the same pony, then they had to dismount and remount to show how well behaved the ponies were.

"We should ask the steward if we could use Cameo," Kelly said, excited all of a sudden. "Then I can double with you!"

Vicki paused to think. "I guess she'll be fine. What could go wrong?"

Kelly could think of a million things, but was too excited to worry about that now. Rushing back to the truck she quickly bridled Cameo, before giving Vicki a boost onto her back. School Pony was her favourite class, and although they'd only ridden double on Cameo that one time on the farm, Kelly was sure she'd be quiet enough.

"Jump on behind me," Vicki said as she rode Cameo up alongside the ramp of the truck. Kelly gingerly climbed onto Cameo's back, sitting behind Vicki, and when the mare showed no signs of objecting to the extra weight, she reached forward and gave her a pat.

"Can I hop on, too?" Amanda appeared around the side of the truck "I reckon we'd win if we had three people riding her. I just checked and no one else has three people on one pony!"

"That's assuming Cameo doesn't buck us off," Kelly said. "You know not many ponies are happy to have three riders on their backs."

"Stop imagining the worst," Vicki said. "Jump on, Amanda."

Amanda slipped in front of Vicki and perched precariously on Cameo's withers, gripping her mane to stay balanced. She was so excited to be riding in the Junior ring with her two big sisters she could barely contain her excitement.

"Stop wriggling," Vicki growled as she guided

Cameo towards the gate. The steward wa...
the riders in. When the judge glanced thei...
Amanda lifted her hand in a wave and Ke...
suppressed a groan.

"Trot on," the steward called.

"Hang on tight," Vicki warned. "If it's going to
go wrong it will be from us bouncing around at the
trot. That mainly goes for you, Kelly, since you're at
the back."

Kelly was nervous now; around them the ponies
were picking up speed, and she gripped her arms
tightly around Vicki's waist. Within seconds Cameo
had moved into a smooth trot, and as they circled the
ring Kelly let out a deep breath. It was the first time
Cameo had been off the lead rein in a competition,
and she was behaving impeccably.

With pricked ears, she followed the pony in front
of her around the circle a few more times until the
judge called everyone into the centre of the ring to
line up. Now came the hardest part: dismounting
and then remounting without assistance.

"Let's do it exactly the same as we used to on
Cardiff," Vicki said, referring to the lease pony she'd
had before Dandy.

But Cameo is bigger," Amanda said.

"And we've never practised on her," Kelly said. "What if she gets a fright?"

"Do you want to win?" Vicki whispered.

Three riders went before them. The first two ponies were well behaved, standing still as their riders clambered off and back on again. The third pony swung around nervously, twitching an ear and backing away from its riders. In the end, the steward had to step forward and help them back on.

Kelly's stomach was swimming again as the judge turned her attention to Cameo.

"Your turn, girls," she said, clipboard in hand.

Vicki nodded, nudging her sisters to remind them of her plan. Kelly slid off backwards over Cameo's tail gracefully, her smile widening when Cameo didn't kick her.

Next, Vicki lengthened Cameo's reins to let her eat. As soon as the mare's head was lowered, Amanda slipped down her neck, landing in a tumbled heap in the grass.

Last but not least, Vicki began her dismount, standing up on Cameo's back and jumping off sideways.

Kelly was filled with pride as the mare didn't even flinch.

Crawling on her hands and knees, Vicki ducked under Cameo's stomach, then knelt beside her shoulder so Amanda could climb up and jump onto Cameo's back. Next, Vicki stood so Kelly could give her a leg up. Now they just had one more rider to get on.

"Grab my hand, and put your foot onto my boot," Vicki said as she held out a hand for Kelly.

It took a few attempts, since Cameo was bigger than they were used to. In the end Vicki had to drop both reins so she could pull and tug Kelly into place, but finally she was settled behind her sisters.

Relieved that they had managed to all remount, Kelly glanced at the judge to make sure she'd been watching. The dark-haired woman shook her head in disbelief, then gave them a smile before moving down the line to judge the remaining riders. When everyone had finished, the judge looked over her notes and then her gaze found Cameo.

"Can I please have the dark grey as the winner," she said. "She would have to be one of the most tolerant ponies I've ever seen."

Amanda shrieked with happiness, and Kelly and Vicki couldn't stop grinning. Cameo had just won her first class, and it was even more special because they'd won it together.

# Chapter 7
# The Golden Girl

IN THE WEEKS FOLLOWING THE Ribbon Day, Cameo continued improving in leaps and bounds. Kelly began working Cameo in the front paddock, teaching her to be soft and responsive as they transitioned between paces. Flatwork wasn't Kelly's favourite thing, though, and after ten to fifteen minutes of schooling her pony, she was ready to have some fun.

"Does anyone want to play cowgirls and Indians?" she asked her sisters. "Cameo and I are bored trotting around in circles."

Vicki shook her head. "Dandy's making really good progress. I want to spend a little longer working on his trot-to-halt transitions."

"Charlie and I will play," Amanda said eagerly. "Can we paint our ponies, too?"

Once Cameo and Charlie were covered in colourful stripes and handprints, the ponies worked up a sweat chasing each other around the paddock, and Kelly and Amanda were soon exhausted, too. Laughter pealed out across the paddock as they made their way back to the house.

"I can't wait for the school holidays to begin," Kelly said breathlessly. "We'll be able to play with our ponies all day long."

It was almost dark as the girls put their ponies away, then detoured to feed their pet rabbits, guinea pigs and birds. Tired and hungry, they went inside for their own dinner.

"Girls," Mum said as they sat down, "guess who's coming to stay for the school holidays?"

Kelly looked up. Mum sounded excited.

"Caitlin?" Amanda said hopefully, referring to her best friend.

"Nope, guess again." Dad grinned.

"I hope it's the Bennett family," Kelly smiled. The girls always had fun adventures with them.

"Wrong again," their mum said. "Nana, Grandad and Uncle Simon are coming to stay, and Simon's bringing his girlfriend, Leah, to meet the family."

"Really?" Vicki asked, suddenly interested. "Isn't she a really good show-jumping rider?"

"The one who was in the *Horse and Pony* magazine?" Kelly gasped.

"Yes, that's the one," Mum replied with a wide smile. "And she's bringing her best horse, Showbiz, with her!"

"When do they get here?" Kelly asked, at the same time as Vicki excitedly asked, "Do you think she'll let me ride Showbiz?" and Amanda said, "Can we take her for a ride at the beach?"

"Calm down, girls," their mum said with a laugh. "They arrive on Saturday. I'm sure Leah will be more than happy to help you with your ponies — but don't overwhelm her on the first day!"

The next few days were spent preparing for their guests, and there wasn't a single spare moment to ride. Every afternoon after school they cleaned the house, tidied the property or mucked out paddocks. Normally Kelly begrudged the endless work that coincided with their grandparents' visits, but as she helped her mum weed the vegetable garden on Saturday morning she couldn't help but whistle.

"What's got you in such a good mood?" Mum asked.

"I'm so excited to meet Leah," Kelly said. "I can't believe they'll be here this afternoon. I really hope she likes us."

"Of course she will," Mum said, digging up potatoes for dinner. "That reminds me, we better head down to the house and make up the beds. You girls can sleep in the horse truck so there's enough room for everyone else."

While Vicki and her mum changed the sheets on their bunks, Kelly and Amanda went in search of flowers to put in the vases on the bedside tables. In no time at all their little bedroom was ready for the visitors, and Mum breathed a sigh of relief.

"Good job, girls. Thanks so much for all your help."

"How far away are they? It feels like years have passed since we found out Leah was coming," Kelly said.

"Any minute now," Dad said, glancing over at the clock on the wall. "Simon said they'd be here at 2 p.m."

"Let's go out to meet them!" Amanda cried. "Should we ride our ponies up the driveway and wait on the road?"

"Great idea," Vicki said. She rushed for the door, tripping over a chair in her haste to get outside.

"It's a five-hour drive, so they're unlikely to arrive exactly on time," their dad cautioned.

But nothing could change his daughters' minds. They caught their ponies and rode them down the driveway to the letterbox, where they sat quietly on their mounts, letting them eat the long grass that grew at the road's edge. Time dragged by and finally they had to admit their dad was right.

"They could be ages away," Kelly yawned.

"It's only a quarter to three," Vicki said, checking her watch. "Let's wait fifteen minutes longer."

"They're here!" Amanda yelled, jolting Kelly from her drifting thoughts. Looking up, she saw a car and trailer approaching with Uncle Simon behind the wheel and waved frantically. He drove slowly past with a toot of the horn. Kelly turned Cameo and trotted down the driveway after them, her sisters not far behind.

Nana and Grandad got out of the car, and the sisters quickly dismounted to hug them. Next was Uncle Simon. They each gave him a distracted high-five, looking past him for Leah.

As Leah emerged from the car, Kelly was struck by shyness. Leah looked exactly like the riders in the magazines. Her long, strawberry-blonde hair was tied in a ponytail, and she wore jeans and a pair of riding boots.

"Hi, girls, it's so nice to meet you," Leah said with a warm smile. "Those are cute ponies. What are their names?"

"This is Cameo," Kelly said, stumbling over her words. "She's four years old and she's only been ridden for about two months. Vicki and I have been training her."

"She's gorgeous," Leah said as she ran her hand down Cameo's blaze. Moving on, she stood in front of Vicki. "What about yours?"

"I'm Vicki, and this is Dandy."

"He looks like a smaller version of my horse, Showbiz," Leah told her with another dazzling smile. Carrying on, she bent down to say hello to Amanda. "You're pretty young to be riding," Leah said. "Tell me about *your* pony."

"I'm Amanda and I'm five and three-quarters," Amanda said, "and Charlie and I love jumping."

"Well, you're in good company, because Showbiz and I love jumping, too," Leah announced. "How about I unload him so you guys can meet him?"

The girls quickly tied their ponies up, then rushed back to watch as Leah backed Showbiz off the trailer. The striking chestnut gelding towered over their ponies, and Kelly had to tilt her head back to look up at his chiselled head.

"How big is he?" she asked in awe.

"He's 16.2 hands, but don't let his size fool you," Leah said with a chuckle. "He's a gentle giant."

One at a time, Vicki, Kelly and Amanda stepped forward and stroked Showbiz's shoulder, which was as high as they could reach. It wasn't until he lowered his head to look at her that Kelly was able to scratch him between the eyes.

"He's got a kind face," Kelly said as she studied him.

"Yes, he does," Leah agreed. "He's such a fun horse to ride, too. I can't wait to take him out on adventures with you all."

"We're going to the beach with the ponies tomorrow," Kelly said excitedly. "I'm taking Cameo for the first time. Would you like to ride out with us?"

"I'd love to," Leah said as she bent over to remove her horse's travel boots.

# Chapter 8
# The Beach Ride

KELLY AND HER SISTERS WOKE early the next morning to catch their ponies. Cameo greeted Kelly at the gate, her kind eyes watching with interest as Kelly pulled a carrot out of her pocket. Slipping the halter over Cameo's head Kelly led the pony down to the yards and tied her up while she grabbed some brushes. By the time she was finished grooming her pony, Kelly was covered in grey hair.

Leaving their ponies tied up with a slice of hay, Vicki, Kelly and Amanda hurried into the kitchen for breakfast.

"Is everyone coming today?" Kelly asked.

"Grandad, Dad and I are staying here," Uncle Simon said. "We have a surprise planned for you girls, and we have some work ahead of us to make it happen!"

"What's the surprise? Tell us," Amanda begged.

"No way, but I promise you'll be jumping for joy when you get home and see what we've made," their dad said.

"So everyone else is riding except Nana?" Kelly said.

"Yes," their mum said. "We'll put Cameo in Leah's horse trailer with Showbiz, then Dandy, Charlie and Jude can go in the truck. That way there's space for everyone."

Looking at her nana, Kelly sized her up. She knew her grandmother had hunted and show jumped in her younger years. "How long since you last rode, Nana?"

"Oh, it must be about twenty years now," Nana replied.

"Cameo's really quiet — would you like to have a turn riding her at the beach today?" Kelly offered. "She's big enough for you."

"Come on, Nana," Vicki urged. "It's a great idea! We'd love to see you ride."

"I'm not so sure," Nana said.

"Aren't you too old to ride?" Amanda blurted out, looking at Nana's grey hair.

Turning to Amanda, Nana thought for a few seconds, then her weathered face broke into a beautiful smile.

"Actually, I don't think I'm too old at all. I'd love to ride, Kelly. Won't that be an adventure!"

∪ ∪ ∪

Riding Cameo at the beach was everything Kelly imagined it to be. The young mare didn't even hesitate when they had to cross the estuary, and when they rounded the point and Cameo saw the waves crashing on the ocean beach for the first time, she pricked her ears and gained a bounce in her step. Kelly was careful to keep Cameo at a walking pace, so Nana could keep up on foot, and Mum and Amanda also stayed with them while Vicki and Leah cantered ahead.

"I think she's ready for you now," Kelly said, dismounting. Mum hopped off Jude and legged Nana up; the older woman swung gracefully into the saddle, sitting in a perfect position. As she took hold of the reins there was no doubt she had spent the first four decades of her life on a horse.

"Tell me something about your riding days," Kelly asked her curiously as they continued down the beach.

"I was riding horses long before I could walk," Nana said. "I used to ride to school, back in the day."

"What about when you were older?"

"My father, your Great-great grandpa Tombleson, and his friends were the very first men to show jump in New Zealand. I grew up competing during the summer and hunting in the winter. We even had a racehorse that won the New Zealand Grand National Steeplechase a couple of times, and Grandad played polo as well. So it's no wonder you girls love to ride — horses are in your blood," Nana said with a smile. "Cameo actually reminds me of a steel-grey mare I used to ride. Her name was Symbol."

"Was she as quiet and beautiful as Cameo?" Kelly asked.

"She was very special, one of my favourites. But she wasn't always easy."

"Did you ever get scared riding?" Kelly asked, listening closely for her nana's answer.

"My father told me it takes a hundred falls to make you into a great rider," Nana said. "Every time I fell off, I'd dust myself off and climb back on my pony, convinced I was a better rider because of it."

Their talk was cut short then by Vicki and Leah riding back to join them.

"Would you like to go for a canter, Nana?" Vicki asked.

"Oh my," Nana laughed. "I'm quite happy just walking! You weren't even born the last time I rode a horse. I'm going to be stiff and sore tomorrow as it is."

"Oh, come on, Nana," Amanda begged her. She and Charlie had just caught up. "You can canter with me."

"I suppose I could do a few strides," Nana finally said, graciously admitting defeat. "Will Cameo behave for me, Kelly?"

"She will," Kelly said grinning. "I bet you'll love it so much, you'll want to start riding again."

With a chuckle, Nana picked up a trot, then quietly urged the mare into a canter as she followed her granddaughters down the beach to the rocky cliffs at the end. Dandy, Jude and Showbiz soon drew ahead, but Cameo and Charlie kept the same steady pace. Lagging well behind them on foot, Kelly shaded her eyes to watch as Nana turned Cameo around and the group began to canter back up the beach towards her. Although there was over sixty years' difference in their ages, Kelly couldn't help but notice that Nana and Amanda wore the same joyful expressions on their faces.

"You looked like a natural," Kelly called to Nana as the riders slowed to a walk beside her.

"That was the most alive I've felt in twenty years," Nana said as she recovered her breath. "I forgot how much I loved to ride!"

"You cantered much longer than a few strides," Amanda said proudly. "You're almost as good as Vicki."

Once the ponies were unsaddled, they tied them up and darted over the road to the dairy to order fish and chips for lunch.

"Uncle Simon said you show jump with Showbiz,"

Vicki said to Leah while they waited for their food. "How high does he jump?"

"We compete in the Amateur Rider series, but we're hoping to do our first 1.30 metres this season."

Vicki gazed at Leah in wonder. "I jumped 95 centimetres once on Dandy. I thought that was big enough!"

Glancing over to Kelly and Amanda, Leah asked, "What about you two?"

"I did 75 centimetres on my old pony, Twinkle," Kelly said. "But I've only done about 60 centimetres, jumping over a log, on Cameo."

"I jumped the same log on Charlie," Amanda said proudly. "And Mum said that was bigger than Kelly or Vicki jumped when they were my age."

"That's really impressive," Leah exclaimed. "I wasn't even jumping at your age!"

"Maybe I'll grow up to be a top show-jumper like you, too," Amanda said.

"I hope so," Nana said. "You and your sisters can keep the family legacy alive!"

# Chapter 9
# Learning the Basics

AFTER THEY HAD TUCKED INTO their lunch, the girls loaded their ponies and they all headed home along the winding gravel road. As they turned into their driveway, Kelly knew she would never forget her first beach ride with Cameo, and spending the day with Leah and Nana.

As soon as the ponies were back in their paddocks, everyone went to see what the men had been up to. They found them still hard at work by the shed. Dad and Uncle Simon were welding something, and Grandad was sawing long, skinny tree trunks into matching lengths.

"Give us half an hour," Dad said, chasing them off. "We'll come find you when we're done!"

The girls took Nana and Leah to visit the aviary. Soon budgies rested on their shoulders, and baby rabbits and guinea pigs snuggled in their laps while they fed them grass.

Dad appeared at the doorway. "We're all ready for you now," he said. Vicki, Kelly and Amanda put their pets down immediately, and followed him as he led them in the direction of the river paddock, with Nana and Leah following close behind. It was clear that they knew what the surprise was, and couldn't wait to see the girls' faces.

"Why are we going this way?" Amanda asked.

"Just wait and see," Dad said as he opened the gate to let them through.

With a gasp, Kelly stopped dead. In the paddock in front of them stood two jumps, an oxer and a crossbar, just like the ones they jumped over at Pony Club and Ribbon Days.

"Real jumps!" she squealed. "With jump stands and everything!"

"Uncle Simon learnt how to weld the jump

stands," Dad explained. "It was his idea. Grandad and I have been helping."

"What about the poles?" Kelly asked, as she took a closer look at the rustic rails.

"They're young poplar trees," Grandad explained. "We felled them, then cut them all to the same length. Do you like them?"

"They're perfect!" Vicki said. "Can we practise jumping over them tomorrow?"

The next morning the girls rode their ponies to the paddock with their new jumps. Before this they'd only been able to train over logs or random objects they'd made into jumps at home, and all three sisters were excited that they now had real jumps.

To double their excitement, Leah had offered to give them a lesson.

"Let's start with some flatwork to warm up," she said, leaving Showbiz at the fence.

She stood in the centre of the paddock to watch the girls and their ponies walk, then trot in a circle around her before calling them to a halt.

"Do any of you know how to work a pony on a contact, so they understand how to soften to the bit?" Leah asked.

The girls looked back at her blankly.

"What is a contact?" Amanda asked in confusion. "And how can a bit get soft? It's made of metal."

"Can't we just jump?" Kelly said, also a little disappointed.

"It can be fun, I promise," Leah laughed, when she saw Kelly's doubtful expression. "Now, hold your reins evenly and apply a gentle pressure, then as soon as your pony lowers its head, even a fraction, you need to soften your reins."

Not really sure what she was doing, Kelly pulled on the reins too hard. Cameo backed up in confusion.

"No, no," Leah said. "Don't pull back on the reins, just a firm but gentle hold."

Trying again, Kelly applied pressure on the reins, but Cameo ignored it, stubbornly refusing to drop her head.

"I think she's falling asleep," Kelly said in frustration. "She doesn't even care."

"She's just confused because she's never been

taught," Leah said. "Here, let me try."

Standing beside Cameo, Leah put one arm over the mare's neck and took the reins. Soon Cameo lowered her head, and Kelly watched as Leah instantly moved her hands forward to release the tension in the reins. "There, you see?" she explained.

Amanda and Charlie were next, then Vicki. Dandy soon understood what was being asked of him.

"Well done," Leah told the girls proudly. "Would you like to try on Showbiz, so you can feel what it's like at the walk?"

Kelly was first, and she couldn't help but laugh at how small she felt astride the giant horse. The ground seemed very far away. With Leah's instructions, Kelly soon had Showbiz working on the bit, softly stretching through his neck and jaw.

"He's so responsive," Kelly marvelled.

"When a horse is trained properly you shouldn't need to pull or seesaw on their mouths at all," Leah explained. "You should just need a light pressure on the reins."

"One day I'll have Cameo working this softly on the bit," Kelly vowed.

"I'm sure you will," Leah said. "Why don't you practise everything you just learnt with Cameo, while Vicki and Amanda have a turn on Showbiz."

Back on Cameo, Kelly listened closely as Leah instructed Vicki.

"Excellent, Vicki," Leah said as they circled the paddock. "Now let's try a trot."

Even though Vicki was bareback, and each of Showbiz's strides covered twice as much ground as

Dandy's, Kelly noticed that her sister barely moved on the horse's back. Showbiz listened to Vicki closely and he was as well behaved at the trot as he had been at the walk.

# Chapter 10
# Jumping for Joy

"THAT WAS THE BEST!" AMANDA exclaimed as she clambered off Showbiz. "But please can we try out the jumps now?"

"Sounds fun," Leah said, when she saw Kelly and Amanda's pleading faces. "Vicki, would you like to jump Showbiz, seeing as you rode him pretty well?"

Thrilled, Vicki quickly dismounted and passed Dandy's reins to Leah.

Leah adjusted the height of the jumps and they approached a small oxer set at 20 centimetres. It was Cameo's very first time jumping over poles, and

Kelly's heart was in her mouth as they wiggled into the small jump.

"They're kind of like logs, aren't they, girl?" Kelly chatted to Cameo, relieved she hadn't refused or run out at the jump. "Nothing to be afraid of!"

Higher and higher the rails went, Leah raising them each time they jumped clear. With each successful attempt, Kelly and Cameo's confidence grew, and soon they were cantering into the jump. Before long the oxer was higher than the log they'd jumped on the farm.

"It looks really big," Kelly said hesitantly. "Do I have to do it?"

"Cameo's been jumping well," Leah encouraged her. "You haven't even tipped it yet. I have a feeling she's going to fly over this height."

Kelly approached the jump with renewed determination. As Leah had predicted, Cameo didn't hesitate, clearing the jump with plenty of room to spare.

But, next time, when the jump got raised to 80 centimetres, Kelly was adamant it was too high.

"I've never jumped that high in my life. I'll just watch."

"Just one more jump," Leah said smiling. "Then, even if you jump it clear, I'll let you finish."

Shaking her head, Kelly refused to budge.

Amanda piped up. "I've never jumped that big either, but if I clear it on Charlie will you at least try it?"

Kelly eyed her younger sister. "I guess," she finally agreed, though her heart was now racing in her chest so fast she thought she was going to be sick.

She watched in disbelief as Amanda cantered into the oxer and her plucky little pony soared over.

Leah clapped her hands together. "Good job, Amanda. You two were flying!"

Amanda beamed, giving Charlie a big pat on his neck.

Now it was Kelly's turn. She took a deep breath and slowly let it out. If her five-year-old sister could clear it on Charlie, who was tiny in comparison to Cameo, then surely she and Cameo could do it too.

Picking up her reins, she urged Cameo into a canter and circled around to the oxer. She squeezed her legs against Cameo's side and the mare flew over.

Kelly's face broke into a delighted smile. She couldn't believe how easily Cameo had jumped it, and felt silly for being so scared. "That was so much fun! I'm not doing any more, though," she told Leah.

"That's the highest we've ever jumped, too!" Amanda said as she rode over to join them. "Can Charlie and I finish as well?"

"Of course! You should both be proud of yourselves," Leah smiled. "That was impressive riding."

Reliving her final jump over and over in her mind, Kelly barely noticed the jump increasing in height as Vicki continued to ride.

"Do you think we'll be able to jump that high when we're eleven years old?" Amanda asked, jolting Kelly from her thoughts. Glancing up, she watched in awe as Vicki cantered Showbiz into the huge oxer, clearing it effortlessly.

"You just jumped 1.2 metres," Leah said in disbelief, "and bareback, too! I think that's a good finish."

"Really?" Vicki gasped. "I didn't realise it was that big!"

"I did!" Leah said with a shaky laugh. "But I knew you could do it."

"Thank you so much," Vicki said. "Now I'll have

so much confidence jumping Dandy — the jumps are going to look tiny."

While Vicki cooled Showbiz down, Kelly and Amanda rode their ponies over to the oxer to have a closer look. The rails were higher than Charlie!

"Even when I'm eleven, I'm not even sure I'd want to jump that big," Kelly admitted.

"I'd like to," Amanda said firmly. "I have six years to practise, so there's plenty of time."

"Rather you than me," Kelly grinned.

# Chapter 11
# A Chance to Compete

THE GIRLS SPENT THE LAST week of the school holidays with Leah, practising everything they had learned. Most days Leah gave Vicki and Kelly a lesson on their ponies, and both Dandy and Cameo had improved by leaps and bounds. Amanda sometimes joined them, but mostly rode around having fun with Charlie.

"You girls will have to enter an A&P Show," Leah said proudly as she watched the ponies trotting around the paddock, working softly on the bit. "You look like professionals now!"

"Are they much like Ribbon Days?" Kelly asked.

"Yes, just bigger and more prestigious," Leah explained.

"What classes do they have for horses?" Vicki asked.

"There are flat and hunter classes — the ponies jump over walls, brush and wire jumps around the outside of the ring. Like at Ribbon Days, but the jumps are much higher," Leah explained. "Then often there will be show jumping and show hunter classes as well."

"It all sounds really fun," Vicki said. "That can be our aim — to compete at an A&P Show one day."

"There's local shows you can enter, then the top riders go down to Auckland to compete at the Royal Easter Show — I'll be there show jumping with Showbiz this season."

"I don't know if we'll ever be that good," Kelly shrugged. "Cameo's just a bush pony."

"Never say never," Leah said with a smile. "Growing up I never thought I'd be show jumping at this level, but look at Showbiz and me now. You'll be amazed what you can achieve if you work hard for it."

That night at dinner, Leah told the girls she'd been talking to their parents and had a surprise for them.

"We've only got a few more days left together, and I think we should do something to celebrate everything you've all learned."

"What are you thinking?" Kelly asked excitedly.

"I checked the calendar of events, and there's a local show jumping and show hunter day on Saturday. I'll be your groom if you are keen to compete."

Vicki's jaw dropped. "Seriously? That would be amazing! But you don't have to be our groom — you should ride, too."

"Well, that's the problem," Leah said mischievously. "I don't have a horse to ride."

"What about Showbiz?" Vicki asked in confusion.

"I was thinking you could ride him."

Speechless, Vicki gaped at Leah, convinced she'd heard wrong.

"You've been riding him so well, I thought you could compete him in the 95-centimetre and

1.05-metre show-jumping classes. Dandy could do the 70-centimetre and 80-centimetre classes." Looking over at Kelly and Amanda, she added, "Cameo and Charlie can enter the show hunter classes, since the jumps will be a little smaller."

"How much smaller?" Kelly asked quickly.

Leah smiled reassuringly. "Show hunter starts at 50 centimetres. Cameo will be fine — you could even trot into them at that height!"

"Fifty centimetres will be easy," Amanda declared.

"You just need to remember that unlike show jumping, show hunter is judged on style rather than speed," said Leah.

"That's lucky, our ponies would never win on speed! Do they have good enough style, though?" Kelly asked.

Leah nodded. "Cameo and Charlie have very good form over the jumps, and they keep a nice rhythm, too, which is important."

U U U

Three days later, Kelly and her sisters were standing

beside the ring, watching as a rider jumped around the colourful set of show jumps set at 1.15 metres. They had an hour until their classes began, and were spending the time learning as much as possible.

"What does 'four faults' mean?" Vicki asked Leah after the horse and rider had left the arena and the announcer had called out their score.

"In show jumping you get four faults every time a rail is knocked down, or a horse refuses at a jump," Leah explained. "The winner is the rider with the least faults, in the fastest time."

Kelly nodded, watching the next rider closely. At the liverpool, a blue tarpaulin filled with water, the horse spooked and pulled off the fence, before approaching again and stopping twice more. "So that's twelve faults, right?"

Leah shook her head. "Actually, three refusals is an elimination."

"There are so many rules! This is much bigger than any show I've ever been to," Vicki said, glancing around. "Look at the huge trucks, and all the beautiful horses."

Kelly couldn't help but agree. "I'd be terrified if I was the one riding Showbiz this afternoon!"

"I am a little nervous," admitted Vicki, as a new horse entered the ring. "But mostly I'm excited!"

A bell sounded from the judges' box, and Kelly watched as the rider picked up a canter and rode through the starting flags, the horse tugging at the bit and bounding sideways as it eagerly flew around the course. She could never imagine jumping Cameo that high, or any horse for that matter.

Back at their truck, the girls quickly dressed in their Pony Club uniforms, while Leah and their parents helped tack up their ponies.

"You really think we can do this?" Kelly asked Leah.

"Of course I do! You guys are going to fly around the jumps. Besides, since it's your first proper show, there are no expectations. Your only mission today is to have fun."

Kelly twisted Cameo's reins in her hands. "So it's all right if we make mistakes, or our ponies misbehave?"

"As long as you're still smiling by the end of the day, then you'll be winners in my eyes," Leah said as she legged Kelly up onto Cameo's back.

With a hesitant smile, Kelly followed Leah to the

warm-up ring, with Amanda not far behind. After the two girls trotted and cantered their ponies around to warm them up, Leah built a small crossbar for them to practise over. From there they progressed to a small upright and an oxer, before Leah called them over to the gate where the rest of their family stood watching.

"You're in next, Amanda," Mum said. "Do you remember which order you have to jump around the course?" Unlike the show jumps, the fences on the show hunter course didn't have numbers to help the girls remember the order of the jumps.

"I think so," Amanda said, as she gathered her reins and rode into the arena. "Wish me luck!"

From the sidelines, many anxious eyes watched on.

"What if she forgets the course?" Vicki asked.

"Then she'll be eliminated, but we've gone over it several times, so hopefully she remembers!"

"What if she falls off?" Kelly asked.

"She won't," Mum said.

"But what if she does?"

"Shhhhh, she's approaching the first jump," said Nana.

Kelly watched closely as Amanda navigated the course, feeling proud of her little sister when she jumped around clear. Charlie, with all of his years of experience, didn't seem to mind the boxes or flowers under the jumps, and he kept a nice even rhythm as he cantered around the course.

"Have fun," Amanda said to Kelly as she rode out of the gate.

Kelly nodded, her face white as she urged Cameo forward.

"Don't forget to walk up and show her the jumps before you start," Leah reminded her. "That way you'll be less likely to have a spooky refusal."

As Kelly entered the ring, she kept reminding herself that today was supposed to be fun. Not only for her, but for Cameo as well. She took her time showing the mare each jump; Cameo just nibbled on the decorations.

"You're a silly girl, Cameo," Kelly said fondly as she picked up a trot. "If you jump everything I'll give you a carrot."

As the mare approached the first fence, her stride faulted slightly, and Kelly had to grip tightly with her legs to keep her straight. The jump wasn't the tidiest, but they made it safely to the other side.

"Good girl," Kelly said as she leant over to pat the mare's neck. Turning, they approached a white upright, followed by an oxer with a little white wall beneath. Cameo was a little uncertain, but with a little kick of encouragement from Kelly, she awkwardly cleared it. Next they approached a line of three rustic brown jumps, with red flowers beneath, and again Cameo bravely attempted them all, knocking down just one rail.

"Only one more," Kelly assured Cameo as they trotted towards the last jump, a grey upright with a box underneath. A few metres out, Cameo slowed, spooking at a dog barking on the sidelines. Worried Cameo wouldn't be able to clear the jump from a walk, Kelly pulled the mare into a circle before approaching it again. To her relief the mare picked up her pace and kept focused into the jump. Up and up Cameo went, clearing it by much higher than she needed to, and it took all of Kelly's effort to stay in the saddle.

As she rode out of the ring, Kelly gave Leah and her family a thumbs-up. She couldn't wait for the next class!

# Chapter 12
# Almost Perfect

"I PLACED FIFTH!" AMANDA YELLED, waving her white rosette as she ran over to where Kelly stood beside the rest of her family, watching Dandy warm up for his show-jumping class.

"That's amazing," Kelly said as she held out a hand for a high-five. "We still have three classes to go, so I bet you'll get lots more ribbons."

"Charlie was so good. Cameo was, too."

"I'm so happy with her," Kelly agreed. "She's going even better than I hoped! Now that she's been over all the jumps, I'm sure she'll just keep improving."

"Vicki's entering the arena," said Nana, pointing.

"She doesn't look stressed at all," Kelly observed as Vicki and Dandy cantered past, focused on the course ahead. "I wish I could be that confident."

Kelly watched with pride as Vicki and Dandy jumped around the show jumps set at 70 centimetres.

"Only two rails," Nana said. "Not bad for a first attempt!"

"Was it as fun as it looked?" Amanda said, running over to the gate as Vicki rode out of the ring.

"Even better," Vicki grinned.

"Come on, girls," Mum called out. "If you don't hurry you'll be late for your next class."

As Kelly mounted her pony, she shivered slightly and glanced up at the sky. A storm cloud was approaching. She hoped the rain would hold off. She was looking forward to jumping Cameo again, and even though the jumps had been raised in height to 60 centimetres, they no longer seemed so daunting.

"You ready?" Amanda asked, as she swung up onto Charlie.

"*So* ready," Kelly said, smiling widely. "I can feel a clear round coming on!"

But by the time they had finished warming up, the heavens had opened. The wind buffeted the jumps, the poles rattling in their cups. In every direction unhappy ponies spun around, trying to turn their heads away from the onslaught. As Kelly waited at the gate she felt like a drowned rat.

"What bad luck," she groaned to her parents who were huddled under umbrellas and thick raincoats. "I wish I could be under an umbrella, too."

"You're already wet through, so what does it matter?" Dad said with a laugh. "You'll be finished in a couple of minutes, then you can hide in the truck until the rain stops."

Fortunately, Cameo didn't seem to mind the stormy weather, and as they trotted into the first fence she pricked her ears, clearing it effortlessly. The second and third were also perfect, and with each jump Kelly's confidence soared. Picking up a canter, she approached the triple line and Cameo kept her rhythm, clearing all three jumps with a beautiful technique.

As Kelly rounded the corner to the final fence, she felt Cameo slip in the slick mud. Her heart lurched as she sought to keep her pony upright, but it was already too late. Cameo's legs skated out from underneath her and Kelly was pitched sideways, clinging desperately to her pony's mane. The ground loomed, there was a sickening thud and blackness engulfed her.

∪ ∪ ∪

Gradually Kelly became aware of her surroundings. Opening her eyes, her vision swam and she heard voices as if from a distance.

Blinking, she began to take in the blurred faces around her.

"How are you feeling?" Dad asked, his voice tight with worry.

"One fall . . . closer . . . to being a great rider," Kelly joked painfully.

Flickering in and out of consciousness, she heard sirens and felt her body being lifted and heard the sound of an engine. Every time she woke, she saw her mum and dad's anxious faces.

Comforted, she closed her eyes again and drifted off.

When Kelly woke up she was lying in the horse truck. Her head throbbed as she carefully pulled herself up into a sitting position.

"Is anyone here?" Kelly whispered.

"Just me," a voice said from beside her.

Turning, and wincing at the pain in her neck, Kelly caught a glimpse of her nana.

"Hey, Nana — what happened? Where's Cameo?"

"Cameo fell over in the mud, but she's fine now," she replied softly. "It's you everyone's been worried about. You've had a concussion. We took you to hospital, and the doctor said you're going to be all right. But no riding for the next three weeks."

Kelly paused for a moment. She was too dazed to feel anything.

"What time is it? And where is everyone?"

"About two o'clock. The rain stopped hours ago and the show's almost finished. I'm just keeping an eye on you while Vicki competes Showbiz in his last class, then we're taking you home."

Kelly went quiet. The fall had been mid-morning,

and she didn't remember most of the day. Exhausted, she closed her eyes and fell asleep again.

υ υ υ

On their way home, Kelly's head had improved enough that she was desperate for an update.

"How did your ponies go?" she asked her sisters.

"Charlie and I got two more placings," Amanda said, holding up three rosettes. "We jumped clear in every round!"

"What about Dandy?" Kelly asked, a hand to her aching head.

"You saw his first class," Vicki reminded her, "then in the 80 centimetres we just had one stop at the wall. The rest he jumped perfectly."

"The real highlight, though, was watching her ride Showbiz," Leah cut in. "She rode him like a champion."

Embarrassed by their praise, Vicki shrugged her shoulders.

"She even won the 1.05-metre class!" Leah added.

"But it didn't count," Vicki mumbled. "The judge eliminated me."

"Why?" Kelly asked in surprise.

"Apparently you have to be twelve years old to compete at show-jumping events on a horse. Anyone younger has to ride ponies."

"Are you kidding?" Kelly said. "So you jumped clear, won the class, then they eliminated you because you were too young?" Her head was throbbing now, but mainly because of how silly it all sounded.

"The judge asked how old I was when she was tying the ribbon around Showbiz's neck. She got such a shock when I told her I was eleven."

"Well, at least you know you won," Nana, ever the diplomat, reminded Vicki. "You don't need a ribbon to remind you of that!"

"I never even thought to check the rules about the minimum age," Leah said, shaking her head ruefully.

"Lucky you didn't!" Vicki exclaimed. "Because, apart from Kelly having an accident, this was one of most amazing experiences of my life."

"I really wish we didn't have to head home this afternoon." Leah said with a pained look. "I feel terrible about your fall, Kelly — I hope you haven't lost too much confidence."

"It wasn't your fault," Kelly said, again rubbing her head. "And it wasn't Cameo's fault either. Besides, I'm one fall closer to being a great rider. Right, Nana?"

"That's the spirit," Nana smiled gently. "I'm proud of you."

"Since you can't ride for three weeks, I can train Cameo for you," Vicki offered. "You won't want her forgetting everything she's learned."

"That would be great, thanks," Kelly sighed. The conversation had tired her out and she was ready to curl up in bed. "It's such a shame we fell. Cameo was jumping a clear round, and I remember feeling on top of the world as we approached that last fence!"

"You'll be back jumping before you know it," Mum reassured her. "Besides, with school starting again, you'll have lots to keep you busy."

# Chapter 13
# Making Do

KELLY'S HEAD SLOWLY GOT BETTER, but she missed being able to ride Cameo. She watched from the sidelines as Vicki took to riding the steel-grey mare once more, teaching her all the things she'd learnt from Leah.

Soon Kelly had something new to look forward to. Vicki returned from town one day waving a sheet of paper.

"Look what Mum and I found at the saddlery," she said in excitement. "The entry forms for the local A&P show! It's only five weeks away."

Reading over her shoulder, Kelly scanned the class list. "The classes are basically the same as a Ribbon Day."

"Just a lot more expensive to enter," Dad said with a frown. He took the forms and quickly read through the rules.

"We can sell some horse manure to help cover costs," Vicki said quickly, clearly desperate to make it work.

"And you can win prize money in every class, unlike at a Ribbon Day, so we might win our entry fee money back," Kelly added.

"Please, Mum and Dad, there's only one A&P Show in town each year," Vicki said, determined. "This is our only chance."

Their parents looked at each other for a moment, and finally their dad shrugged. "I'll advertise that we have horse manure for sale, but be warned, we'll have to collect a lot to help pay for it,' he said.

The next day, Kelly was checked by a doctor and was cleared to ride Cameo again. With the show approaching, she was delighted and relieved to find that she and the pony picked up exactly where they had left off.

"Any nerves?" Mum asked, after Kelly jumped Cameo for the first time since her fall.

"Not as many as I expected," Kelly shook her head in relief. "But for the moment let's keep the jumps low. And I'll try to avoid riding on wet and slippery ground!"

∪ ∪ ∪

The next month flew by, and with each day the girls' excitement grew. Their ponies were schooling better than ever and they were confident that Dandy, Cameo and Charlie would do well at the show.

"Girls, I just talked to another Pony Club mum to find out the difference between competing at A&P shows and Ribbon Days — apparently they're a really big deal," Mum told them one day over lunch.

"That's why we've been training the ponies, just like Leah taught us," Kelly said, confused.

"It's a little more than that," Mum said with a sigh. "There's specific gear you're supposed to have, and you're not allowed to ride in your Pony Club uniforms — you have to wear riding jackets."

"So what are we going to do?" Vicki asked. "Can we afford new riding gear?"

"Even second-hand they're several hundred dollars," said Mum in a strained voice, "and there are three of you. We can barely afford the entry fees, so I'm not sure how we're going to make it work."

"But we've got the ponies going beautifully," Vicki said, "and the show's only a few days away. Surely we'll find something suitable, or maybe Leah will let us borrow one of her jackets."

"Oh honey, she lives five hours away!" Mum said. "I don't think she'd be able to make it up in time, even if she wanted to."

"What about something from a garage sale?" Kelly asked. One of her favourite things to do on the weekends was to wake up early to go bargain-hunting with her dad. It's where they found all their clothes, books and board games.

"It's too late, silly," Vicki said. "The show's this weekend."

"What about the second-hand shop in town, then?" Kelly said, her voice rising in hope. "They might not have riding jackets, but if we find something similar no one will ever know!"

Mum nodded. "Good idea, Kelly! It's definitely worth a try."

υ υ υ

That afternoon, Kelly stood searching through racks of used clothing, looking for a jacket that fitted her.

"What colour are they supposed to be?" she asked.

"I'm not sure," Mum replied. "I never asked that!"

"Well, I've found a pale blue jacket that almost fits." Kelly rounded the corner and twirled to show off a pretty dress jacket, probably worn in its previous life by someone in an office job. "It's only twelve dollars and will look beautiful against Cameo's grey coat."

"I found one, too," Vicki said, as she did up the buttons on a well-worn navy jacket. "Although the sleeves are a little long."

"I can take up the sleeves," their mum smiled. "That's an easy fix. Now we just need something for Amanda."

After an hour of searching, there was still no jacket for Amanda.

"My jacket is the smallest one we've found," Kelly said, passing her pale blue jacket to her little sister. "Why don't you try it on?"

Amanda stood impatiently while Kelly bent down to button it up. The sleeves hid her hands, and the bottom of the jacket reached almost to her knees.

"I won't even be able to reach the reins," she said as she waved her arms around, the sleeves of the jacket flying wildly.

Bending down, Kelly rolled up the sleeves. "I think it looks perfect," she said. "I'll find another one."

# Chapter 14
# Show Time

THE MORNING OF THE BIG show soon arrived. Their gear had been cleaned and the ponies had been washed and groomed to perfection. Even Cameo's stockings were white, after hours of soaping and scrubbing.

When they reached the showgrounds, Kelly looked around in wonder at the carnival rides and people. In the horse area, dozens of beautiful ponies were trotting around a large grass ring. They were immaculately turned out, and their riders wore beautiful tailored outfits. "You've got an hour before the first class starts," Dad said as they unloaded their ponies. "Why don't you get ready, then you can ride around the showgrounds to get them used to everything."

"Great idea," Kelly said, watching a girl prance past on an exquisite black pony.

In half an hour the ponies were tacked up and ready to ride. As the girls circled the showgrounds, Kelly kept a firm grip on Cameo's reins, in case she spooked at a flapping tent or the roller coaster rattling in the distance, but Cameo seemed as calm as ever.

The sisters rode into the Junior Ring to warm up. In every direction riders sat tall and elegant in their leather show saddles, their ponies polished to perfection as they trotted and cantered past.

"This must be your first time at a show."

It was the same girl on the black pony that Kelly had noticed earlier. The three sisters eyed her cautiously. From her velvet helmet to her soft, calf-skin leather gloves, she was impeccably dressed. Her pony gleamed in the sunlight, beautiful plaits gracing its muscled neckline.

"You can't seriously plan to compete looking like

that?" she said, her eyes wide.

"Like what?" Amanda said, her eyebrows lowering in confusion.

"You haven't plaited," the girl said. "The judges will be shocked, that's all."

"It's our first A&P show," Kelly explained, her face bright red in embarrassment. "The rules said nothing about plaiting."

The girl rolled her eyes. "You're just supposed to *know* these things," she said. She turned her pony away, shaking her head. "Honestly."

"Don't let her get to you," Vicki urged. "It's not about how we look, it's about how well our ponies go."

"No, it's not," Amanda groaned. "It's like a beauty pageant for horses. Our ponies look like they've come straight out of the bush."

"They kind of have," Kelly said, with a shaky laugh. "We should at least plait their manes though — we'll have time if we hurry."

Cantering back to the truck, they hurriedly tied their ponies up.

"Mum, would you help us plait our ponies' manes?" Kelly called urgently.

"What kind of plaits?" Mum asked as she stepped out of the truck. "I've never plaited a pony in my life!"

"We looked at some of the other ponies. It looks like they just divided the mane into heaps of sections. Then the sections were plaited all the way down to the ends, and the plaits were rolled up into little balls," Kelly said.

"We don't even have any rubber bands. Let me go see if I can borrow some," Dad said, disappearing between the line of trucks.

He returned a few minutes later and joined in the frantic efforts.

"Kind of like this?" he said, pointing to Charlie's neck.

"Normally a little tidier," Kelly said with a frown. "But better than no plaits at all."

Cameo and Dandy were soon plaited, too, although their plaits weren't much better.

"All this effort, just to win a ribbon," Mum said. "Seems a bit silly, really."

"You'd better get back to the ring," Dad said. "Otherwise you'll miss your classes and you'll have plaited for nothing."

As Kelly rode Cameo to the gate, she lifted her spirits by chatting away to her pony, telling her how fun the day was going to be.

"When the judge sees how sweet and quiet you are, they'll love you," she assured her.

But to Kelly's dismay, it wasn't to be. The judge paid no attention to Cameo in their first class, or in their second or third, and Vicki and Amanda weren't doing any better. It soon became obvious that their ponies were not only the worst presented, but also some of the least trained in the ring. While Cameo and Dandy were the best they'd ever been, they lacked the consistency of the more experienced show ponies, and Charlie was even more out of place.

"I don't think we belong here," Kelly muttered. "I much prefer Ribbon Days!"

"Doesn't it inspire you to get better?" Vicki asked as she glanced around the showgrounds. "One day I'm going to win against these types of ponies, and I'm sure you and Amanda will, too."

"The next class is Novice Rider, and all three

of you are entered. Make sure you keep your heels down and thumbs on top," Mum instructed. "And don't forget to smile!"

Sitting a little straighter in the saddle, Kelly focused hard on her position, determined to ride her best. As she walked, trotted and cantered around the ring, she let the world fall away and focused instead on everything Vicki and Leah had taught her.

"Second place to the rider on the dark grey," the steward called out. Kelly's breath caught as she glanced at the judge in disbelief. Steering Cameo into the middle of the ring, Kelly did a double-take when she saw Vicki already lined up.

"Did you win?" Kelly whispered as they waited for the judge to decide on the rest of the place-getters. "I was so busy concentrating on my position I didn't even notice the judge call you in!"

"I guess so," Vicki said, as she patted Dandy proudly.

"Can I please have the young girl on the little grey in fourth place," the judge called, pointing to Amanda.

"Are you sisters?" the judge asked as she tied the blue ribbon around Cameo's neck. "How old are you all?"

"Vicki's eleven, I'm nine and Amanda is almost six," Kelly answered shyly.

"Well, I think you all ride brilliantly." The judge patted their ponies. "I hope you keep showing. You're naturals."

"She said we're naturals," Kelly gushed to her parents when they rode out of the ring. "Maybe I like A&P Shows after all."

# Chapter 15
# Pony Makeover

ONCE SCHOOL WAS OUT FOR the summer holidays, they had plenty of spare time to fill in, and they were committed to finding out how to present their ponies properly for the show ring. Determined to do better next time, and to have their ponies looking the part, the girls begged their mum to take them to the library so they could borrow some horse books.

"We need to learn as much as possible so we're not the odd ones out next time," Vicki told her mum.

"It's OK to be different," Mum reminded her gently.

"That's not what's bothering us," Kelly said. "We just want to learn as much as we can, so we can give our ponies the best possible chance."

Later that afternoon the sisters were in the non-fiction section of the library with a pile of books.

"What are you looking for?" Mum asked her daughters, picking up a book and flicking through the pages.

"We're going to give our ponies a makeover, but first we need to figure out how," Kelly said.

"What's wrong with them?" Amanda asked, a little offended on behalf of Dandy, Cameo and Charlie.

"According to this book, nothing scissors and a pulling comb can't fix," Vicki said with a smile.

The next day Kelly and Amanda stood beside their parents as they watched Vicki snip, snip, snip. Hair fell from their ponies' scruffy jaws and legs. She even cut about 10 centimetres off the bottom of the ponies' tails, so they were in line with the bottom of their chestnuts, the little knobbly growths on the inside of their hind legs.

Next she wrapped each of the ponies' long manes around a comb and tugged heaps of hair out, until they were short and tidy. By the time she had finished, all three ponies were virtually unrecognisable.

"Dandy no longer looks he was born in the mountains," Vicki said in awe.

"And Cameo doesn't look like a common street pony," Kelly whispered.

"Even Charlie looks like a fancy show pony," Amanda said, unable to believe her eyes.

The girls ran their hands over their ponies, almost as if to confirm they were indeed the same animals. Cameo stretched forward to nuzzle Kelly, and Dandy stamped a hoof as if impatient with all the fussing.

"Their manes will be much easier to plait now," Mum said as she ran her fingers through Cameo's pulled mane. "No wonder the show ponies had such small, even plaits!"

A few days later, their Dad came home from a garage sale with a box of old equestrian magazines, and Kelly and her sisters spent hours reading through articles and looking at photos.

"I found an article that shows us how to plait properly!" Kelly said in excitement.

Turning the page, she continued reading,

astounded to see step-by-step instructions on how to apply dark makeup to accentuate a horse's bone structure, and how to brush quarter-mark patterns onto their rumps.

"Makeup!" Amanda exclaimed in shock, when Kelly showed her. "Why do they need makeup?"

Excited by the prospect of learning as much as possible, Kelly and her sisters put into practice everything they read in the magazines and books. Every day they plaited their ponies until it became effortless. Their first attempts were clumsy, and it took over an hour to manage a few plaits, but after a week they were able to finish their ponies' entire manes in under forty minutes.

Next they bought a stencil from the saddlery shop and spent their afternoons learning how to brush quarter-mark patterns onto their ponies' rumps, and lastly they used their savings to buy a pot of black horse makeup.

The first time they tried applying it, Cameo ended up looking like a panda. Kelly and Amanda howled with laughter when they saw the mess Vicki and their mum had made. Finally, after a few practice runs they found the makeup added to their ponies' beauty rather than making them look a million times worse.

"I think that's as good as we're going to get," Mum said one day, as she looked over Cameo's subtly applied makeup.

Nodding in agreement, Kelly admired the perfectly presented ponies. "I think we're ready for another show."

# Chapter 16
# Finishing Touches

"YOUR PONIES LOOK INCREDIBLE," LEAH said as she admired Dandy, Cameo and Charlie when she and Uncle Simon came up to visit during the last week of the summer holidays. "And you've done such a good job training them over the past few months — they're working beautifully."

"Thanks, Leah," Kelly said proudly. "We've been practising everything you taught us!"

"I think you would hold your own down at the Royal Easter Show in Auckland," Leah said as she watched them trotting on a circle, working softly on the bit. "It's only a couple of months away now!"

"Really?" Kelly said doubtfully. "You realise we made total fools of ourselves at the last show, right?"

"You didn't make fools of yourselves," Leah shook her head adamantly. "But you've come a long way since then. There's no comparison between the wild kids I first met four months ago and the three young ladies and their noble steeds standing before me now."

"Now you're just being silly," Amanda giggled.

"In all seriousness, I really think you're ready, even if you just enter the novice classes."

"I'll talk to Mum and Dad," Vicki said. "I don't know if we'll be able to afford it, but I'd really love to come, even if it's just to watch you and Showbiz competing in the show-jumping classes!"

That evening, Vicki broached the subject, and Leah pulled out the programme so everyone could see what classes there were. To Kelly's surprise, their parents took very little convincing, quickly agreeing that the girls could compete.

"We've really admired how much time and effort you've spent this summer training your ponies," Dad said. "It will be a fun weekend away and a good learning experience, if nothing else."

"But if you thought the local A&P Show was a shock after competing in Ribbon Days, then the Royal Easter Show is at a whole other level," Leah warned. "Your riding's up to scratch and your ponies look the part, but there are a few tweaks you could make to your outfits and saddlery."

"What's wrong with it?" Kelly was dreading the answer. She'd known their gear hadn't been as smart as the other competitors at the A&P Show, but none of them could quite pinpoint what was missing. And even if they knew what was wrong, Kelly wasn't sure they had the money to change it.

"Nothing, if you were just doing the jumping classes. But for the flat classes at royal level, you'll need a sheepskin saddle blanket and show browbands made of ribbons to match your outfits. That reminds me," Leah said. "I brought up some old gear you can have."

She headed outside, returning with a box filled with a tangled mass of leather.

"There's a couple of nice bridles in here. They just need a good oiling."

Kelly untangled a browband covered in faded

and fraying ribbons and held it up. "Is this what you mean by a show browband?" she asked, carefully running her fingers over the orange, cream, brown and gold ribbons woven together to form a shark's tooth pattern, with decorative rosettes on both ends.

"Yes, that's what you need," Leah said with a smile. "Just a little less tattered."

U U U

The next day, after Leah and Uncle Simon had left to go home, the girls' parents took them into town to visit the saddlery, with a list of items Leah thought they needed, including hair nets to keep their hair tamed, gloves, and jodhpur clips so their jodhpur pants wouldn't slide up and show their socks while they were riding.

"I've found browbands," Vicki said, "but you're not going to believe how expensive they are!"

"How much?" Dad said as he walked over to have a closer look.

"A hundred dollars each!" Vicki said. "That's twice what it cost to buy Dandy."

"I'm sorry, kiddo, but there's no way we can afford that," Dad said. "And I've just found the saddle blankets, too, which are even more expensive."

"That's OK," Vicki said glumly, exchanging looks with Kelly and Amanda. All the sisters knew their parents would have bought them if it was at all possible.

"I might have a solution," Kelly spoke up. "I was studying Leah's old browband yesterday. If we buy some ribbon and buttons, I'm pretty sure I can make them for us."

With renewed hope, they headed to the fabric store to look at ribbons.

"Leah said the browbands have to match our outfits," Kelly said. "So we need pale blue and navy for Amanda and me."

"And red, navy, white and gold for me," Vicki said.

Soon they had metres of the many different coloured ribbons measured out, and had also selected buttons for the centre of the rosettes.

"That'll be eight dollars and thirty cents," the shop attendant told them, and the girls smiled delightedly at each other.

Later that evening, while the rest of her family sat around reading, Kelly carefully unwound Leah's old browband, taking note of how the ribbons were twisted together so she could re-create it. Finally, she was certain she understood the order and direction in which the ribbons were woven and set about making a new one on a spare leather browband she'd found in the box of odds and ends Leah had given them.

It was even easier than she'd thought, and in less than an hour she had stitched the ends of the ribbons together and glued them in place.

"All done," she said, holding up her creation. "Now I just have to work out how they made the rosettes."

Carefully, Kelly cut and pried one of the rosettes loose, until little pieces of ribbon, plastic and buttons sat scattered on the floor around her. After studying it for ten minutes she was sure she could copy it.

"Mum, Dad — would you help me for a bit?" Kelly said as she carefully threaded a needle.

"Hang on a second," Dad said as he sat on the ground, snipping something with scissors. Turning, he held up a crudely cut sheepskin. "Your Kiwi ingenuity inspired me to think outside the box! I made each of you a saddle blanket."

With a gasp, Mum dropped the book she was reading. "You cut up our beautiful rugs!" she said, horrified.

With a shrug, Dad grinned. "We can get new rugs one day, but right now the girls needed sheepskin saddle blankets."

There was a flurry of activity to sew everything in place according to Kelly's instructions. Soon the rosettes were finished.

"Dandy's browband is done," Kelly said with a yawn. It was well past her bedtime. "I'll work on Cameo's and Charlie's tomorrow."

Dropping her book, Vicki rushed over to look.

"It's amazing," she said. "It looks just like the ones in the store!"

"There's even enough matching ribbon left over to tie in your hair," Mum said. "You girls are going to look like show riders after all!"

# Chapter 17
# Diamonds in the Rough

ALL TOO SOON EASTER WEEKEND was upon them. With the ponies washed, their saddlery oiled and their riding outfits organised into sets, they packed the truck and loaded the ponies. The three-day Royal Show would be the first overnight event the girls had ever attended, and the three-hour drive was the furthest they'd ever travelled with their ponies. Their dad took extra care driving on the crowded motorways, and Kelly held her breath as she looked down at the sea, far below, as they crossed the Auckland Harbour Bridge.

From the moment they pulled into the showgrounds they were caught up in the hustle and bustle of finding a car park, registering at the office and settling the ponies into their assigned stables. Everywhere they turned there were gorgeous horses, and Kelly went from stall to stall admiring them. Most were covered from head to toe in thick rugs, hoods and leg wraps; some only had their eyes, ears, nostrils, knees and hooves visible.

It wasn't until they reached the final horse that Kelly realised what made them look so different.

"They've had their whiskers shaved off," she gasped. "And all the hair's been clipped out of their ears."

"They have, too," Vicki said, as a leggy grey nuzzled her hand, its muzzle closely shaven. "Poor things — they must feel so disorientated without their whiskers. Remember when our instructor at Pony Club told us that horses use them to help sense where they are?"

"That's right," Kelly said, remembering. "Especially at night, when their eyesight's not so good."

Moving on, they circled back to their own ponies to check their hay and water.

"Do you think our ponies will mind being locked up?" Kelly asked Vicki as they tossed a deep bed of straw onto the floor of the stables.

"I don't know. Cameo and Charlie have never even been yarded before," Vicki said with a frown, "and Dandy hasn't been confined since his early days out of the wild."

Worried that the ponies would feel cramped in their stalls, the girls led them out to the grass oval to let them graze for as long as possible. By the time they put them to bed for the night, the stables were long abandoned.

"Why don't we ask Mum and Dad if we can sleep with our ponies?" Amanda said. "That way we can keep an eye on them."

Half an hour later, the three girls were setting up beds in the narrow area beside their ponies' stables, normally used for storing hay and wheelbarrows. The spare bales of hay they'd brought made a hard bed, but the thought of sleeping in the stables was so exciting Kelly didn't mind.

Curling up in her blanket, she lay awake talking to her sisters, waiting for the stable lights to turn off. Beside them, their ponies shuffled restlessly.

"Maybe the lights stay on all night?" Kelly finally said at midnight.

"Our classes are early tomorrow morning," Vicki said with a yawn. "We probably should try to sleep."

UUU

Kelly was woken at 6 a.m. by a stream of people checking on their horses. In every direction there was someone either washing, plaiting or feeding their mount. A few gave them curious looks as they walked past, surprised to see three sleepy faces peering back at them from under the blankets.

"Did you sleep in the stables?" a girl about Amanda's age asked.

"It was fun." Amanda yawned as she pulled hay out of her curly blonde hair.

"If you don't mind sleeping on a hard bed of hay," Kelly added as she stretched the kinks out of her neck.

"You're weird," the girl laughed. "I'd better be going."

A few minutes later Kelly heard the little girl's

voice again, "It's true, Mum," she was saying. "They slept in the stables, just like Cinderella."

Giggling quietly, Kelly grabbed her blanket and followed her sisters back to the truck. It was a good comparison!

U U U

The morning went past in a mad dash as the girls prepared for their classes. Time was running out, and they had stalls to muck out, ponies to feed and manes to plait.

After eating a hurried breakfast, they returned to the stables with their parents to groom and plait their ponies. Standing on a bucket, Kelly carefully separated Cameo's mane into even sections, then dampened the hair with a wet sponge so it would be easier to plait.

"Where are all the other kids?" she asked. Looking around, she could see only adults, mostly mums, grooming ponies.

"Maybe they're still sleeping?" Amanda said.

"Perhaps they're used to their parents doing

everything for them," Dad suggested. "Unfortunately for you, girls, you already know more about presenting horses than the two of us combined."

"We offered to teach you how to plait," Vicki reminded him as she bent to oil Dandy's hooves. "You weren't interested."

"Look how well that turned out for me," Dad said with a smile. "I get to sit here watching while you do all the work."

Once their ponies were groomed to perfection, the girls led them down to the truck and tied them up, leaving their dad to saddle up while they changed. The outfits that they'd first bought at the second-hand shop were now complemented by new ties which matched their browbands. Their mum tied matching ribbons at the ends of their braids.

"Now we look the part," Kelly said with a decisive nod.

"Let's go warm the ponies up," Vicki suggested. "They'll need to stretch their legs after being locked up all night."

After circling the oval at a brisk trot, the girls found the right warm-up ring and rode in among the crowd of ponies. It was far more chaotic than they were used to. Ponies were going in every direction, with some being ridden while others were lunged on long leads. Luckily their ponies didn't mind the commotion and worked quietly.

"Can we please have the riders for Novice Pony on the Flat, Under 138 centimetres, zero to three wins?" the gate steward called.

Across the warm-up arena, Kelly caught her sisters' eyes. "That's us," she said nervously.

"Just pretend you're riding in the paddock at home," Vicki reminded them as they entered the ring. "Forget about the other ponies and the judge."

It was easier said than done, though. As they joined the other ponies in the ring, Kelly checked out the competition, struggling to keep her focus on her pony. Ahead of her was a striking chestnut mare, and opposite, a young boy rode a pretty palomino. Kelly's mind continued to wander, and she accidently pulled on the reins in her distraction. Cameo swished her tail and chomped on the bit in agitation.

"Sorry, girl," Kelly said as she softened her hands, trying to regain her focus. Soon Cameo's strides evened out and she relaxed, working softly on the bit just like they'd practised. Smiling, Kelly settled in and enjoyed the ride, no longer concerned about the other ponies in the ring.

"Canter on," the steward called out.

With a squeeze of her heels, Kelly asked Cameo to increase her pace. As Cameo cantered around the ring with her ears pricked forward, like a real show pony, Kelly thought about how far Cameo had come. It seemed impossible that just eight months earlier she'd been tied to a rusty old truck, being led through town.

The judge began to call out the place-getters. First, a striking bay mare and rider were called in, and then the boy on the palomino.

"Can I please have the dark grey?" the judge called out.

Kelly was surprised to see the judge pointing at her. Slowing Cameo to a walk, she turned into the centre of the ring and proudly stood while a yellow ribbon was tied around Cameo's neck.

"We placed third," Kelly sang in delight as she joined the others. "The judge liked Cameo!"

"You rode so well out there," Mum said proudly, as they made their way back to the stables. "Who would have thought, when you first got Cameo, you'd be winning a ribbon at the Royal Easter Show in your very first year together?"

Glancing over at Leah, who'd joined them, Kelly smiled her thanks. "Leah did, right from the beginning. And so did Vicki — she kept believing in me even when I wanted to give up."

"You were all diamonds in the rough," Leah said, as she gave Kelly a hug. "You just needed a little polishing."

# Chapter 18
# Collecting Ribbons

By LUNCH TIME, ONCE THE novice flat classes were done and dusted, many ribbons fluttered from the back of the horse truck.

"I'm so proud of you," Mum said, giving them each a hug.

"Cameo and Dandy were almost unrecognisable out there," Dad said. "They fit right in with the purebred show ponies, and I heard rumours that some of those cost tens of thousands of dollars!"

"What about Charlie?" Amanda protested. "He did well, too."

"He was a champ," Dad said fondly. "Not many other ponies would behave so impeccably with such a young rider on board."

"Everyone else your age is down there in the Lead Rein ring," Mum added, pointing to the far corner of the showgrounds.

Grinning, Amanda shook her head. "There's no way I could keep up with my sisters if I was still on the lead rein!"

With their classes done for the day, Kelly followed her family over to the show-jumping ring to watch Leah compete Showbiz. The course was set at 1.30 metres, and the pair was like poetry in motion as they flew around the jumps.

"I wish I could look that effortless, over jumps half that height," Kelly said wistfully.

"Leah's been riding her whole life," Mum reminded her. "I bet when you're her age you'll be just as good!"

Smiling, Kelly imagined her older self. Would she show jump like Leah and Showbiz, or tame wild ponies like Vicki had done last summer? Maybe she'd still be competing in the show ring, or just ride for fun on the farm or at the beach. One thing she did know for sure, though, was that she would still be riding — like Nana had said, horses were in her blood.

∪ ∪ ∪

The next morning shone bright and clear as the girls rode their ponies bareback around the hunter ring to show them the jumps. As Kelly gazed around at the ponies warming up, she couldn't help noticing the mixture of horses that were competing today.

"The hunter classes seem much more relaxed," she observed to her sisters. "Even before our makeover we would have fitted right in."

When they reached the brush jump, Cameo snatched the tea-tree branches in her mouth, destroying the perfectly trimmed hedge. "Cameo!" Kelly cried out in horror, glancing sideways to see if anyone had noticed.

"At least it's smaller now," Amanda said.

"Smaller is good," Kelly giggled as they rode back to their truck. "I'm so glad we're only in the novice classes."

"How are you feeling, after seeing the size of the walls and the brush?" Mum asked.

"Dandy will fly around them," Vicki boasted.

"I'm surprisingly confident," Kelly added as she loosened Cameo's girth. "I've decided to spend the day pretending I'm brave."

"Fake it till you make it, huh?" Dad grinned. "I like that plan."

"What about you, Amanda? Think Charlie will make it around?"

"Shhhh!" Amanda covered her pony's ears. "Of course he can do it. Charlie would be hurt if he heard you doubting him."

"That's good," Dad said, "because we bought you each a present with the prize money you won yesterday." He produced three large parcels from out of the truck.

"They're all the same," Mum warned. "So make sure you open them at exactly the same time."

The girls all took their presents excitedly. Kelly was just opening hers when Amanda squealed.

"Jumping boots!"

Kelly hurriedly ripped the paper, pulling out a pair of her very own. She held them up excitedly before bending down to put them on Cameo's legs. "Thank you! Now she looks like a real jumping pony." She gave her mum and dad a hug each.

∪ ∪ ∪

An hour later, Kelly rode out of the ring in a buzz. She'd just finished her first hunter class on Cameo, and it had gone better than she'd ever imagined.

"A clear round," she gasped in delight as she hugged her pony, "and we didn't even trot!"

"That was a dream round," Leah said rushing over to join her. "I arrived just in time to see you jump!"

"All the hard work's been worth it," Kelly acknowledged. "That was the best feeling in the world!"

"Don't get too comfortable — there's plenty more to learn. For starters, I'd better show you how to put on jumping boots correctly!"

"Seriously?" Kelly said in dismay as she dismounted and checked the boots on Cameo's front legs.

Leah checked Dandy and Charlie's boots before doubling over in laughter. "You're all wearing them upside down and back to front!"

Mortified, Kelly and her sisters watched as Leah demonstrated how to put them on correctly, and their parents crowded around to learn as well.

"I can't believe we competed like that and no one pointed it out," Kelly moaned. "How embarrassing!"

"Mistakes are never bad, as long as you're willing to learn from them," Leah said with a reassuring smile. "I bet you'll never put jumping boots on the wrong way again!"

"That's for sure," Kelly said with a smile, and bent down to practise.

# Chapter 19
# The Grand Parade

As KELLY RODE INTO THE ring for the last time she paused, taking in all the people standing on the sidelines watching, and shook her head in wonder. It still didn't feel quite real competing at one of the biggest shows in the country.

These were her final moments in the ring, and she meant to savour them. As she and Cameo flew over the first three fences, Kelly focused on her position, careful to keep her heels down, thumbs on top and hold the reins just as Leah had shown them. It was her rider class, and although it was important that the ponies jumped clear, she knew the judge was looking to see how well she rode. Looking up, she approached the red wall, turning and soaring over the double brush jumps before slowing Cameo to a halt and saluting the judge.

As she left the arena Vicki flashed her a smile. "Cameo keeps getting better and better every round. She looked like a pro out there."

"Dandy, too," Kelly said as she replayed the round in her head, elated with how well it had gone. "I still can't believe you won the last class! And you've qualified for champion hunter."

Kelly waited for the final riders to compete. Amanda was among them and she watched proudly as her little sister jumped a perfect clear round.

"That right there is what showing is all about," Leah said, as Vicki and Kelly congratulated Amanda on her ride. "Those smiles are what makes you all winners in my eyes. You should be very proud of yourselves."

While they waited for the results to be announced, Vicki quickly mounted Dandy to begin warming him up. The judging for Novice Champion Hunter would begin as soon as the current class winners were announced.

"The winner of Novice Rider Over Hurdles, Under Ten Years is Kelly Wilson on Cameo," the announcer called out. "Second place goes to Amanda Wilson and Charlie Brown."

Kelly looked at her sisters in disbelief. She couldn't believe they'd finished first and second in a hunter class, especially over such big fences!

Thrilled, Kelly rode Cameo into the ring to collect her ribbon, Amanda following just behind.

"Thanks, Vicki," Kelly said, once she'd returned from their lap of honour and jumped down from Cameo's back.

Startled, Vicki looked at her sister. "What did I do?"

"Thank you for helping me train Cameo," Kelly said. "Also for making me try new things, even when I was scared. This has been the best weekend of my life and it wouldn't have been possible without all your help with Cameo."

"It was fun," Vicki said as they rode back to the truck. "Cameo is the very first pony I've started under saddle completely by myself, so it was one of my highlights, too!"

∪ ∪ ∪

"The steward said you'll all be required for the Grand Parade," Mum said, hurrying over to the truck. "It starts in five minutes and we need to tie all the ribbons you've won around the ponies' necks!"

"But I let Charlie roll," Amanda said.

Pausing in mid-stride, Mum looked over at the filthy pony and groaned in despair. "Argh, of course you did!"

"Why don't you double behind me?" Kelly asked as she grabbed the ribbons she'd won.

Soon Cameo had a blue and a yellow ribbon tied around her neck, and Kelly had a red one across her chest to show everyone it was won in her rider class. Amanda, who sported a blue ribbon, sat on Cameo, perched behind the saddle.

Dandy's neck was graced with ribbons of every colour, with the purple sash for Novice Champion Hunter tied in pride of place. Vicki also was covered in ribbons, with a red and blue one crossed over her chest.

When they reached the arena, almost a hundred horses and ponies milled around while a steward put them into order.

"You'll be at the front, with the rest of the champions," he said to Vicki, sending her and Dandy forward. Kelly and Amanda joined in with a group of riders towards the back.

As the procession started, Dandy took the lead, pacing out proudly. Crowds gathered to watch as the horses walked in pairs around the showgrounds, showing off the ribbons they had won. On and on the line went, until finally Cameo bought up the rear, Kelly grinning broadly while Amanda waved wildly to the onlookers.

Some of the other horses shied or jig-jogged at the commotion, but Cameo strode quietly on. In comparison to trotting through traffic, the Grand Parade wasn't overwhelming in the least.

# Cameo

Cameo, with her sweet and kind nature, was one of our favourite childhood ponies.

As a foal she was black with a blaze and four white stockings, and over the years she faded to a steel-grey, then a dapple-grey, until finally she was completely white! Born in 1993 in the Far North of New Zealand, in 1997 our mum spotted her trotting through the main street of Kaitaia, tied to an old rusty truck.

Cameo stood at 13.2 hands and for many years was right in the middle of all our adventures. She enjoyed farm and beach rides as well as Pony Club and competitions. She was a highly successful all-rounder with many wins at A&P shows, dressage formation rides, cross country, show hunter, show-jumping and games competitions.

You will meet Cameo's good friend, Casper, in the next book in the Showtym Adventures series, as well as read all about Dandy and Cameo's ongoing adventures!

# Characters

**Vicki** has always shown talent for riding, training and competing with horses. She has won national titles and championships in Showing, Show Hunter and Show Jumping, and has represented New Zealand internationally. Dandy was the first pony she trained, when she was nine years old, and then twenty years later she won the World Championships for Colt Starting. When she's not riding, she loves to learn as much about horses as she can, from farriers, vets, physios and dentists.

**Kelly** has always been creative. She loves horses, photography and writing. Although she competed to Grand Prix level when she was sixteen, she now only show jumps for fun, and also enjoys taming wild horses. Her favourite rides are out on the farm, swimming in the river, or cantering down the beach. When she's not on a horse, she is very daring, and loves going on extreme adventures.

**Amanda** is the family comedian and can always make people laugh! As a child she was always pulling pranks and getting up to mischief. Amanda began show jumping at a young age, and competed in her first Grand Prix when she was twelve. In 2010, she won the Pony of the Year, the most prestigious Pony Grand Prix in the Southern Hemisphere, and since then she has had lots of wins up to World Cup level. When she's not outside training her horses or teaching other riders, Amanda loves doing something creative — she has already filmed two documentaries and is writing her first book.

**Mum** (Heather Wilson) grew up with a love of horses, although she was the only one in her family to ride. She volunteered at a local stable from the age of thirteen, teaching herself to ride when she was gifted an injured racehorse. Although she rides only occasionally now, her love of horses hasn't faded over the years, and she is always ringside to watch her daughters compete. In her spare time, Heather loves painting and drawing anything to do with horses, and as 'Camp Mum' is popular with the young riders who attend Showtym Camps.

**Dad** (John Wilson) grew up with horses, hunting, playing polo and riding on the farm. His family also show jumped and trained steeplechasers, so he has loved horses from a young age. He hurt his back when he was in his twenties, which has limited his horse riding, but he enjoys watching his daughters ride and is very proud of their success. When he's not fixing things around the farm, he can be found gardening or creating stunning life-sized horse sculptures from recycled horseshoes.

# How-tos

The most important thing about owning a pony is to learn as much as you can about their care and training, so you can make their life as fun and easy as possible! In each book in the *Showtym Adventures* series, we will expand on key lessons Vicki, Amanda and I learnt on our journey to becoming better horse riders. Some lessons we learnt by making mistakes; others from observing our horses and learning from them — and some knowledge has been passed down to us by others. We hope you enjoy these top tips!

## How to sew plaits for the show ring

The thought of plaiting your pony might seem daunting at first, but with a little practice it will become part of your competition routine. Here is a step-by-step guide to get perfect plaits that will be admired in the show ring.

## Before you begin

Make sure your pony's mane is pulled to an even length and that you have everything you need:

- rubber bands and thread (these should be the same colour as your pony's mane)
- a blunt needle
- scissors
- a mane comb
- water (either applied with a spray bottle or with a sponge).

To reach your pony's mane comfortably you may also need to stand on a plastic box or steps. It is also useful to have someone to hold your pony for the first few times that you plait, to ensure your pony learns to stand quietly.

## Plaiting in 10 easy steps

1. Wet the mane. Using a mane comb, divide the mane into equal sections and secure each section with a rubber band. There are no rules about how many plaits you should have down the neck, provided it looks balanced, although an uneven number is traditional.

2. Start plaiting at the poll. If your pony becomes restless during the plaiting process, it's easier to finish off plaits near the withers than those near the ears.

3. Divide the section of mane into three equal portions and plait all the way down to the ends. As you plait, try to keep the tension even. Each plait should be firm, not loose, and this can only be achieved by keeping your thumbs on top while you plait.

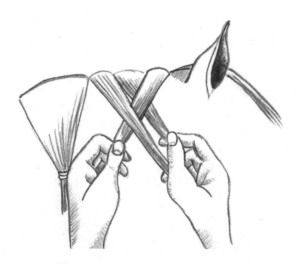

4. Hold the bottom of the plait tight with one hand while you use the other hand to bind it. Twist the rubber band around twice, turn up the strands at the end of the plait, then finish binding with the rubber band to keep all loose hairs secure. If your pony shakes its head and you let go at this stage, you will have to start again.

5. Thread the needle and pass it through the rubber band at the base of the plait from front to back. Fold the plait in half, turning the end under, then pull the needle through from underneath, near the base of the mane, to come out on top. Make a couple of stitches down the folded plait, following the zigzags made by the hair sections so the stitches are hidden, so that the needle comes out at the bottom.

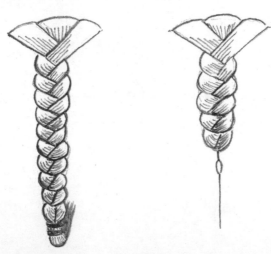

6. Finally, fold the plait in half again, putting the needle through from underneath near the base of the plait and stitch backwards and forwards three times to keep the plait secure. Knot the thread underneath the plait, and trim off the loose ends with scissors.

7. Stand back to admire your handiwork, but don't be tempted to pull out any stray hairs that have escaped or you'll eventually end up with a spiky and uneven mane.

8. Repeat the process all the way down the neck. Each plait should be roughly the same size, although the plaits near the withers might be slightly smaller. Your finished plaits should be firm to touch, not loose. The secret is to make the initial plait tight, which is by keeping your thumbs on top as you plait. It is worth practising at home to get this right — and it also gives you an opportunity to thin your pony's mane further if the finished plaits are not dainty enough.

9. Next plait the forelock using a French-style plait. To do this, divide the top of the forelock in three and plait as normal for a few turns, then take in a small section of hair from each side every time you cross over. Bind with a rubber band, then fold under and sew as normal.

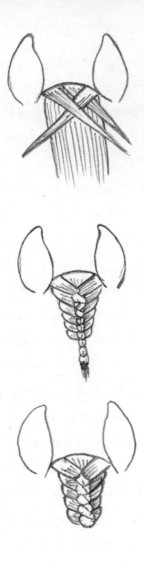

10. Spray the plaits with hair spray, if needed, to keep stray hairs in place.

# Thank you

WRITING CAMEO'S BOOK HAS BEEN so much fun, taking me back to a time I once thought of with embarrassment. Growing up, there were many times where a lack of money meant we had to do without, or had to make do with cheap or second-hand clothing and gear. While it was never something I noticed in my early years, it was often a source of mortification as a teenager.

Now, though, I can appreciate just how important our early years were in developing our character and Kiwi ingenuity. We learnt to make do with what we had, or to create ways to overcome setbacks. Our constant desire to make the most out of life motivated us to work hard, strive for excellence, and eventually overcome both our financial and our social situations.

Our biggest thanks goes to our parents. Although we lived in a tiny house, with furniture and sheets hanging from the ceiling to divide the rooms initially, had to shop at garage sales and struggled to afford the bare essentials, you were always willing to do whatever it took to support our love of horses. We appreciate the many sacrifices you must have made over the years, and are especially thankful for you helping us find a way to make our dreams a reality, rather than seeing all the reasons why they were most likely impossible. We grew up seeing possibilities, not problems, and I think that has been a vital mindset in everything we have achieved since.

Of course, many of these dreams wouldn't have been possible without Vicki. From a young age she encouraged us to dream, and then showed us over and over again that those dreams could come true. It is only by her example that we came to realise that we were not defined by who we were, rather by what we wanted to become. Her relentless quest for self-improvement, followed by the countless hours she spent passing on everything she learned, is why we are the riders we are today. Thank you for believing in us and investing your time into us — we appreciate everything you have taught us over the past twenty years.

As young riders, although we couldn't afford instructors, there were often times that special people came into our lives and offered such insightful knowledge that we will never forget them. Leah was one of these people, although I'm sure those two weeks spent at our property during the school holidays or the times she visited in the years that followed don't seem as significant to her as they were to us. The passion she instilled in us, and the lessons she taught us, were fundamental in developing us as riders.

A few years ago we were unexpectedly reunited with Leah when her daughter attended our Showtym Camps; although two decades had passed, we recognised her straight away! That encounter was very special to us — a chance to thank her for everything she did for us as children, and to reflect and reminisce over bittersweet childhood memories. We were very saddened to hear of her passing recently, and hope she looks down from heaven and sees what her legacy has left behind. She is the star of this book, and one of the many catalysts for our successes since. None of us would have believed that Vicki's very first show-jumping class on Showbiz would eventually develop into a full-time career with horses, or that she would go on to win show-jumping events at World Cup level.

Lastly, I would like to thank the team at Penguin Random House for their belief in the *Showtym Adventures* series. When they first approached me about writing stories for children, I was a little hesitant; originally the plan was to write a fiction series with Vicki, Amanda and I making guest appearances as instructors. Having only written true-life stories, with the purpose of educating people about the plight of wild horses, it seemed a little trivial to write fiction, and I struggled to outline where the books would go, or what I was trying to say.

After a lot of soul-searching I realised our own childhood had so many lessons to teach people, so I set about recounting the special ponies and life lessons that made us into the people we are today. Through the process I have gained a greater appreciation of our parents and the way we were brought up — I am so thankful to the foundations they gave us in our early years.

So thank you Debra, Catherine, Diana, Jenny and the rest of the team at Penguin Random House for instigating this series and setting me on this journey of self-discovery. You have been a joy to work with, and I always appreciate your wisdom and insight during the editing process — these books are better because of you. I have loved reliving our adventures with Dandy, Cameo and Charlie, and can't wait to see where the rest of the series takes me.

Coming next . . . Don't miss Book 3 in the
*Showtym Adventures* series

# CASPER, THE SPIRITED ARABIAN

Vicki's biggest challenge yet . . . to transform a dangerous pony!

When Vicki hears about a difficult Arabian that no one wants, she will stop at nothing to save him. Years of misunderstanding have left Casper wayward and mistrustful, but Vicki senses a gentle soul beneath the pony's rough exterior.

Vicki must learn the importance of patience and compromise to have any chance of winning over the high-strung gelding. Will Casper ever trust humans again? And will Vicki be able to uncover the potential she sees in the spirited Arabian?

This story of self-discovery and second chances, in which Vicki, Kelly and Amanda Wilson first help a misunderstood pony to trust again, is inspired by the Wilson Sisters' early years.